Tell Slash B
Hell's A' Comin'

Elliot Long

D1345424

A Black Horse Western

ROBERT HALE · LONDON

© Elliot Long 2016
First published in Great Britain 2016

ISBN 978-0-7198-1991-9

The Crowood Press
The Stable Block
Crowood Lane
Ramsbury
Marlborough
Wiltshire SN8 2HR

www.crowood.com

Typeset by
Derek Doyle & Associates, Shaw Heath
Printed and bound in Great Britain by
CPI Antony Rowe, Chippenham and Eastbourne

For Gaia June
A loved Great Granddaughter

Tell Slash B
Hell's A' Comin'

Mort Basset – the powerful owner of the Slash B ranch –
thinks he and his men have got away with the killing of the
Cadman family, when the corrupt Broken Mesa court finds
them not guilty. But Basset and his men soon find that this is
not to be. The men involved in the murders begin to be
hanged or shot dead by an unseen avenger, and they soon
find that the man they are after is a deal cleverer than they
anticipated, and the killings continue. Where will it end?

CHAPTER ONE

Mort Basset, aggressive-looking owner of the Slash B, was not in a happy mood as he rode his chestnut gelding and brooded his way across South Range. There had been a complaint made by Ryan Caldwell, owner of the Diamond C, situated twelve miles west – out there on the Dyson River. Slash B cattle had broken down Diamond C fences and were now grazing on Diamond C land.

Mort spat his spent chaw into the sun-dried grass. Well, he'd dealt with the complaint. Slash B fence wire was now mended and Slash B cattle had been driven back on to Slash B land. But, dammit, at one time, and not that long ago, there was no wire on this range and Ryan Caldwell wouldn't have given a rat's ass about cows wandering, knowing full well matters of who owned what would be settled come round-up time. Mort scowled. Another thing was biting at his gut: he and his men still had fifteen more miles to ride before they reached Slash B headquarters, situated north, close by the deep-running Cold Iron River.

More wrath filled Mort. Damnation, it was bad enough

7

having those sonsofbitches nesters complaining about straying cattle, but now Ryan Caldwell was beginning to protest. . . . Mort sighed deeply. Well, things just weren't the same any more, and that was a bald fact.

He stared around at the seven hard-faced men riding with him. He shouldn't be here; dammit, he shouldn't. Usually South Range was a place he visited only when there was a drive for market, or for spring and fall round-up and branding. All other times his line riders kept an eye on things. So once more, damn all sodbusters. They were directly or indirectly the cause of all the trouble on this range and the terrible things that had recently befallen Mort Basset personally these past couple of years. He didn't give a hoot in hell if people thought otherwise. Those sonsofbitches farmers had been trouble ever since they showed their ugly faces on this range, waving their bits of government paper and fencing off what they claimed was their land.

Barbed wire! It was Satan's own invention and, like most ranchers in this basin, he had developed a real hatred of the stuff and for those soil-grubbing bastards who brought the curse of it into the valley.

Why, almost from the first day those government-backed sonsofbitches arrived in Broken Mesa, the county seat, pulling their rickety carts or steering their creaking wagons, or just came plain walking in with their large, gaunt and hunger-thinned families strung out behind them, they'd spelt trouble. What was even worse, they didn't seem to give a hoot in hell about the beeves that ripped their hides on those needle-sharp barbs, or for the fly-infested sores that developed because of those wounds. Why, at times those injuries even led to death and that, decided Mort, was a real big assache.

He continued to stare fiercely ahead, his thoughts still nagging at him like individual rivets being driven into his head. For, indeed, not satisfied with that, those bastards seemed to want to further humiliate the ranchers by having the gall to say that they had no real cause to complain, for most of them had not paid a red cent for the land they occupied; they were, in effect, trespassing upon government property.

His thinking resting on that bald claim Mort felt every fibre in his fifty-seven-year-old but still well-muscled body once more burn with bright rage at that biting recollection.

Goddamnit! If he'd had his way he would have driven the whole bunch of them right out of Wild Horse Basin soon as they put one goddamned trespassing foot on to it. Or, better still, hung the lot of them from the nearest cottonw—

The faint crack of a discharged rifle sent echoes thwacking into the distant hills. The noise killed his resentments stone dead, and for some reason that he could not yet define hope rose like a beacon within him.

A report like that usually meant one of two things in this territory: men killing game or attempting to kill each other. He turned expectant blue eyes onto his rangy, grey-eyed, tall-in-the-saddle straw boss, Jim Alston, who was riding almost boot-to-boot next to him.

'Y'all make of that, *compadre*?' he said, eagerness in his tone.

Jim had been his good friend, as well as, later, his *segundo*, for nigh on twenty-five years. Indeed, they had been firm companions ever since enlisting with the Texas

9

Rifles to fight for the Confederate cause when the Civil War broke out, 1861. They'd hoped to win. For sure, they did not want those Yanqui bastards interfering in the affairs of the Lone Star state; they could quite capably do that for themselves, by God!

But he soon found things do not always work out the way a man wishes them to and with the cause lost, and along with a few other like-minded Texicans not wishing to live under the heel of those Yanqui bastards, they explored the possibility of starting afresh some place else, even to the extent of turning to outlawry if it came to that. But in their wanderings they discovered something more intriguing: thousands of maverick cattle roaming a war-torn and Comanche-emptied land. The finding was enough to cause the party of eight malcontents he was riding with to pause and raise expectant brows and rub their chins thoughtfully, just as he did. For, no doubt about it, they could pick up a real sizeable herd here by rounding up those aimless on-the-hoof dollars, then head them north to new territory and find markets in which to sell them.

Remembering those stirring times, Mort now looked pleasurably about him, for it was still a pleasure despite the horrendous things that had recently befallen him. This was Wild Horse Basin, so named because of what he and his fellow Texicans found when they arrived here twenty-four years ago: hundreds of feral horses.

Almost gleefully now, Mort remembered what happened after that. They rounded up the horses and broke them to the saddle, then sold them to the Yanqui Bluebellies at Fort Laramie, who were frantically having to build forts all along the Bozeman Road to try and control – though they did not succeed – Red Cloud's Sioux and Dull Knife's Northern Cheyenne, who were staging one big uprising in protest against any further encroachment upon their tribal lands. Even though it galled all of them to sell horses to the Yanquis, at the end of the day the old proverb prevailed: *beggars can't be choosers.*

Snapping him out of his memories which, oddly it seemed, had only taken moments to recall, he heard Jim Alston answering him:

'Sounded like a rifle to me and that ain't usual in this neck of the woods.'

Mort nodded his eager enthusiasm. 'Damned right it ain't,' he said. 'Maybe it's one of those nesters and maybe what we find when we get to where he's at will brighten up what has been, until now, a bastard of a day.'

Jim raised a thin smile, although he wasn't sure whether his friend and boss was being humorous or if he was wallowing in one of those often-murderous depressions that plagued him these days after all his misfortunes. For a certainty, what with one thing and another, these past two years had been pure hell for Mort, and for Jim Alston to a lesser extent, because he'd always considered himself to be an integral part of the Basset family and could feel the pain near as hard as Mort could. Indeed, right from Mort finding his wife Sarah by writing off to one of those marriage bureaus back East and marrying her – because she was so pretty – almost as soon as she stepped down off the Overland coach, he'd always figured himself to be kind of a brother and brother-in-law to the both of them and uncle to the kids they reared.

Crazy, but that was the way he'd figured it to be. Sarah, though she strongly disapproved at first of Jim Alston living in the same house, came round to the idea after Mort's firm insistence that he should. So, yeah, when those two terrible things hit the family two years back he had also taken those tragedies to heart near as bad as Mort had, except for one thing: he did not blame the grangers for what had befallen Slash B – that was solely Mort's crazy reaction.

Jim felt the pain once more. For what did happen to the family was truly horrendous. It had all begun with the murder of Mort's wife Sarah and his two girls, Mandy and Jane by the Sioux, and the rape and horrific mutilation of their bodies afterwards.

Jim closed his eyes. Dear God, that was bad enough, but when those Long Riders killed the boys, Clint, Brazos and Mathew, along with the eight Slash B riders who were helping them drive that herd to Wichita . . . well, from that point Mort's wrath had known no bounds.

Mort blamed the nesters outright for what had happened to his family. He fervently claimed that if they had not come into the basin and distracted him he would have foreseen what could happen to his family and would have taken action to prevent it.

Yeah, thought Jim, right now Mort was plain out of his mind, though it hurt like hell having to admit to that.

To answer Mort, he coughed, pulled down on the rim of his brown, dusty and sweat-greased Stetson and urged his roan gelding into a canter.

'Reckon we'd better take a look,' he said.

'Damn right we'd better,' Mort said.

Jim did not like the eagerness that now gleamed in

12

Mort's intense blue eyes. In fact, he was really disturbed by it. If it was a granger doing the shooting out there, God knew what would happen. . . .

CHAPTER TWO

As they rode Jim worked out the shot had come from the direction of the arroyo that cut a wide, deep trench across this east section of South Range. After five minutes' riding he espied the big brown Morgan horse standing droop-headed and patient, close to the arroyo's rim. Slight concern filled him. He knew that beast; knew its owner. That wasn't good, not with Mort along.

He urged his mount forward that last half-mile. Now at the edge of the dry wash he looked down. What he saw caused his gut to tighten even further and he could not stop the hissed word 'Damn!' that escaped his lips when he realized the more than possible consequences of this find.

It was a prime Slash B steer that was lying dead at the bottom of the arroyo and John Cadman, granger from down by Newton Creek, was standing over it, knife in hand and working on hacking off the rear left haunch, hide and all.

Had Cadman killed the beeve for meat? Jim found he could not accept that. He had visited Cadman recently and figured him to be a peaceful, law-abiding fellow; a man who kept himself to himself and troubled nobody, least of all the ranchers. Jim also knew of other reasons why the nester would make sure he kept his nose clean. He had a sweet, petite, ginger-haired, wife and two fine children: a sturdy boy maybe four years old and a bonny, blonde-haired girl aged around six. The man would not endanger his family by doing such a foolhardy thing as butchering a Slash B beeve right here on Slash B range – not in a coon's age. Or would he?

Mort arrived beside him and stared down into the arroyo. Before Mort could voice his anger, Jim said,

'Easy, old friend; I reckon this ain't what it seems.'

Mort stared at hint 'You figure?' He grinned, but it lacked mirth. '*Compadre*,' he said, 'I got news for you – I reckon it is. What's more, that goddamn son of a bitch is goin' to hang for what he's done this day.'

Jim had expected the reaction but still felt his whole body tighten up.

'For Christ's sake, Mort, ease up now,' he said. 'There has to be a reasonable explanation for this and we got to look into it.'

'A nester, reasonable?' A malicious sneer spread across Mort's square, craggy face. 'Jim, use your eyes. He's shot and killed that steer. That son of a bitch is stone-cold guilty.'

'We don't know that,' Jim said. 'We've got to look into it. Top of that, as well you know, with the grangers rolling in, county law is in the basin now, as well as federal law. Get a grip on yourself, Mort. D'you really want those star-toters nosing into our business if we hang him? Dammit, we've got to take him into Broken Mesa and let Judge Neilson decide.'

Mort spat brown chaw juice into the dust. 'Well, to hell with that,' he said. 'He's broke the rules and he's goin' to pay.'

John Cadman's voice rattled up loud and clear from the bottom of the ravine, clearly taut and nervous. He was staring up at them.

'Hang me, you say? I was passin'; I heard the animal bawling. I climbed down and found it had broken its right hind leg in the fall so I did what any decent man would do, I put it out of its misery.' Cadman then paused and frowned. 'And what rules you talking about? I know nothing about no rules.'

Mort aimed a fat calloused index forger at the granger, his gaze like two bullet heads behind it.

'Rules men have lived by in this basin for nigh on twenty-five years, rules you duck-shit farmers would know nothing about ... or don't want to know. But, by God, mister, you're soon going to find out!'

Slight desperation now filled Jim. 'Mort, I know this man. I reckon he's tellin' the truth. We got to go down there and check out his story. If we discover he is telling the truth we have to let him go. For Chris' sake, get it through your head, Slash B ain't the law on this range any more.'

Mort was staring his disbelief. 'Did I hear you aright?' He waved an arm to take in the surrounding countryside. 'We've been losing stock hand over fist to these bastards ever since they arrived in the basin, and you say let him go now we got proof?' Mort narrowed his eyes. 'You gittin' soft in your old age, old friend?'

His concern for Cadman growing, Jim said, 'It's more likely that some Paiutes from up in the mountains have been taking our beeves. Most of them are half-starved out of their minds these days. And, dammit, you've never minded them taking a beeve or two, as long as that was all they took. You always said: after having taken their land off them it's the least we could do.'

Mort's grooved face gelled into a mask of pure hate. 'Maybe one time,' he said, 'but right now, if I got the chance, I'd skin every last one of those red bastards for what they done to me and mine . . . and the same goes for these damn grangers. They're scum, thieves, all of them.'

Jim sighed and said, 'Mort, it was the *Sioux* that did for Sarah and the girls, not the Paiutes. As for the grangers, you can't mean that. You've got to be crazy to even think that way. Once and for all, get it through your head, you're not the law on this range any more.'

Mort glared, his square face flushing red. 'Did you say crazy? Damn you, Jim, I'm protectin' my own; so should you be.'

Before Jim could make a reply Mort turned to the six still-mounted Slash B hands ranked along the arroyo's rim. He pointed at the nearest two.

'You, Rowdy, Frank; get down there and drag that thieving bastard out of there.' Then he glared along the line to the oldest man in the bunch, situated at the far end of the row. 'You, Bowdy Gleason, get your damned rope ready.'

The oldster spat, raised brows and said, 'Sure thing, Mr Basset. Anythin' you say.'

Meantime, Rowdy Mason and Frank Lawson looked at each other long and hard. Then Rowdy, his brown, range-lean face screwed up in enquiry, said,

'Are you sure about this, boss? I mean, ain't it illegal to hang a man these days?'

Mort's frown resembled a ferocious gathering of black thunderheads. He tapped his broad chest with a horny finger.

'In case you've forgot, Rowdy, *I'm* the law on Slash B range. What I say goes. Now, get down there and get it done, or, by God, you can draw your pay when we get back to Slash B!'

With keen grey eyes Jim watched Rowdy's Adam's apple bob up and down. Oddly, he found he was hoping for some sort of rebellion from the man, but Slash B was one of the best-paying outfits in the basin and, for all his faults, Mort was ranked as tops when it came to looking after his men, so he was not greatly surprised when Rowdy said,

'Gee, boss, no need for that.' Then Frank Lawson added, hastily, 'No, sir. No need at all.'

Mort nodded, a faint sneer on his red face. 'Well, I'm glad to hear it, boys,' he said. 'Now get down there and get it done.'

With a shrug Rowdy and Frank began to climb down into the arroyo. Meanwhile, Bowdy Gleason detached his lariat from its home on the saddle horn and began to wait patiently or further orders.

CHAPTER THREE

As Rowdy and Frank approached Cadman down the side of the arroyo Jim watched the granger's lean features go desperate and jaw-tight tense. Cadman looked what he was – a tall, labour-hardened hunk of a man. What was more, Cadman went into a fighting crouch and raised the bloody knife in his right hand in a stabbing position. He was clearly prepared to defend himself.

Seeing the move, Rowdy paused, drew his Colt .45 single-action, armed it and lined it up on the sodbuster's chest.

'Don't be a damn fool, Cadman,' he said, 'put the knife down.'

Jim watched Cadman's body go even tauter. For moments the granger flicked a gaze at his Springfield rifle, which was leaned against a rock near by. It seemed as though the man was debating his chances of reaching it before being shot down by Rowdy's Colt, or by any one of the six rifles now pointing down at him from the arroyo rim.

But after moments of indecision Cadman dropped his shoulders, threw the knife to the ground and glared up at the men lined up along the top of the arroyo.

'Are you going to let him to get away with this? You heard him? He intends to hang me.'

There was an air of seeming indifference, even expectation, among some of the hands and Jim felt his gut tighten. This was crazy. This could lead to big trouble for Slash B. Worse, Bowdy Gleason was saying, in his slow drawl,

'The thing is, fella, you broke the rules. Now Mista Basset won't allow that. No, sir.' He looked along the line of riders. 'Ain't that right, boys?'

'Ranchers' rules!' Cadman burst out. 'They don't apply any more!' He stared at the line of men. 'For God's sake, boys, try to get the man to see reason; I've done nothing wrong.'

Mort barked, staring at Rowdy and Frank, 'Damn you down there, get that bastard outa there right now, y'hear me?'

Rowdy stared at Cadman and raised his eyebrows. 'You comin' quiet, fella, or are we goin' to have to drag you out?'

Jim saw that cold determination was now filling Cadman's lean features.

'You can try,' he said with calm firmness that now seemed alien to the situation. He clenched his fists, making it clear he was not prepared to quit without a fight. Frank Lawson looked disappointed and shrugged.

'OK, fella, you chose it.'

Rowdy holstered his Colt. Then the both of them went in, swinging hefty punches. Even so, and with apparent ease, Cadman ducked and weaved, easily evading those powerful but clumsily aimed blows.

20

Then Cadman counter-attacked with a more skilful assortment of well-directed blows and Frank and Rowdy, already bloodied by the assault, were forced to back off. Indeed, Frank had a deep, blood-welling gash above his right eyebrow, Rowdy's mouth was seeping blood and Jim saw that a big bruise was already swelling on Frank's right jaw. However, he knew those boys to be tough individuals who had been involved in many a rip-roaring barroom brawl.

Now once more the boys pressed forward, making it clear they were prepared to take a load of punches in order to get through the granger's guard to pound the hell out of him. But Cadman fought like a cornered mountain cat, evading, dodging, and attacking in return. Nevertheless, Frank and Rowdy finally managed to break through his clearly trained defence until he was sprawling on the ground, panting and bloody.

Yet, so violent and draining had the onslaught been that the battered and bloody Slash B boys seemed hardly able to find enough strength to manhandle the gory, scarred and punch-dazed Cadman to his feet and drag him the arroyo's rocky side.

Despite the thrashing Cadman had taken, when the three reached the top of this dry wash he was recovered enough to glare with bruise-pouched eyes at the waiting Mort and say, through bloody and battered lips,

'Damn you, Basset, stop this insanity. I'm innocent I tell you.'

Mort leaned forward, eyelids narrowed.

'You're Cadman, ain't you? That squatter down by Newton Creek?'

Cadman glared. 'I'm no squatter. I paid hard-earned

21

cash for that land and I work it good. What I heard, you and those like you paid nothing!'

Not the right answer, Cadman, Jim thought. He watched Mort's thickset body stiffen; watched the deep-held and unreasonable hatred he now held for the grangers well up in him once more.

'For God's sake, easy, Mort,' he said.

But ignoring him, Mort leaned forward. His look was evil as he said,

'Now listen well, Cadman. Many other good men and women fought and died to possess this basin. We paid for it with our blood, our sweat, and their tears. You on the other hand, and the scum that came with you, paid ten dollars. Now, to me, and all the other men who found and tamed this land, you're not only squatters but thieves to boot, and being a thief you is goin' to hang forthwith – and that's the one damned certainty here.'

Despite being battered and cleeding Cadman reared, erect and defiant.

'You can't do it,' he said. 'You are no longer the law in this basin. If you hang me, you will surely die in like manner – for murder.'

A mirthless smile spread across Mort's square face.

'An' you're banking on that, huh?' Abruptly, he turned to the bloodied Frank and Rowdy. 'Damn you, what in hell are you waitin' for? Get the job done. Hang him!'

But Rowdy Lawson, clearly punched out and hurting, said, lamely,

'We ain't got the rope, Mr Basset.'

Bowdy Gleeson waved the lariat in his hand and grinned.

'Right here, boys. This'll sure do the job. You can lay

22

bets on that.' With apparent calm he slung the lariat over the nearest cottonwood bough that appeared strong enough to bear Cadman's weight. Then he offered another black-toothed grin.

'Better hoist him up on his horse first, boys,' he said. 'Ain't no use him standing on the ground.' Then he raised grizzled brows, and as if wanting to correct some misunderstanding here he added, 'As fer hangin' fer it?'

Bowdy rubbed his chin as if deliberating carefully before continuing. 'Well, boys, I figure Mr Basset here'll see that don't happen. Ain't that right, Mr Basset?'

Mort offered a grim nod. 'Right, Bowdy,' he said. Then he turned and glared at Rowdy and Frank. 'Now will you get it done, goddamnit!'

'Mort, don't do this,' Jim said. 'It'll lead to big trouble, I tell you. We ain't the law any more.'

Mort glared at him. 'Jim, shut your mouth.' Then he turned his attention back to Frank and Rowdy. 'Now do it, dammit!'

The boys tied Cadman's hands behind his back and with the help of others, the granger protesting and struggling violently, they seated him upon his big Morgan horse.

Bowdy Gleason rode close and drew his lariat tight around the granger's thick neck. Battered and bleeding, Cadman stared at the Slash B owner.

'Listen good, Basset,' he said, 'when the Judgement Day comes, as it most assuredly will, you will go straight to hell; I promise you.'

With a roar of rage Mort reared in the saddle. 'Damn you, Cadman, for the thief you are!' he roared. With a curse he swung his quirt and lashed Cadman's big horse across its ample rear – once, twice, three times, while yelling, 'Git, hoss, git!'

The man holding the beast by the bridle out front yelped an oath, let go of the leather and scuttled out of the way as the big animal squealed and reared and then bolted, to leave Cadman swinging in midair, kicking and gagging on the end of the hemp rope.

Piss began pouring yellow out of the bottom of his worn and patched denim trousers. *God in heaven, what have we done?* Jim thought.

CHAPTER FOUR

For stunned moments Jim watched, in raw disbelief, Cadman swing on the end of the hang rope. Jim fought to gain his composure, his mind working overtime. He had to do something, and quickly. There was only one thing to do. He drew his Bowie and urged his horse forward. Glistening in the sun the blade slashed Gleason's lariat apart. Cadman fell in a heap to the ground, but his head seemed to be rolling loose atop his sun-browned neck.

It quickly became clear that the granger's neck was broken and that the man was no longer of this life. With bitter eyes Jim looked directly up into Mort's intense blue gaze and said,

'He's dead. What you got in mind now?'

Mort lifted thick brows and said, as if surprised by the question,

'Why, we burn his damned cabin. Ain't that what we allus do?'

'It ain't worth the matches,' Jim said with acerbic sarcasm.

Mort said, as if amazed, 'It *ain't*?' Then he grinned, revealing strong but yellowed teeth and added, 'Well, it'll be no great loss then, uh, compadre?'

Raw anger flared hot through Jim as he replied, 'Damn you, his wife and kids'll be in there!'

Mort held up a hand 'Whoa, easy there, amigo, somebody'll have told them to get out of there by time we arrive. Sure to have done.'

'The hell they will!' Jim said.

Mort frowned. 'Dammit, they're nesters, Jim,' he said. 'Jees, I never took you for a bleeding heart.'

Jim tried to marshal his thoughts. It was no use arguing with Mort in this mood, but he knew now that he had to do something to stave off yet another tragedy. The idea came to him fast.

'Mort, leave me to handle the rest of it,' he said. 'I'll ride to Newton Creek, tell the widow about her loss. We can't burn her out. She needs a roof and she has two young children to care for. Damn you, man, show some mercy – you're gettin' to have no feelin's at all.'

But Jim knew right off that his plea had fallen on deaf ears as Mort set his face into a grim mask.

'We burn, y'hear?' Mort said. Then he turned and, as if expecting opposition, he stared at the now sullen-faced hands sitting their mounts near by.

'He brought it upon himself, y'hear?' he bawled. 'Now, those that can't stomach the rest of what needs to be done can head on back to the ranch. I'll deal with what pay is due you when I return. Am I making myself clear?'

Nobody moved, but a gravelly voice called from the back.

'Hell, Mr Bassett, ain't we done enough? Jesus, that little lady and her two kids . . . dammit, I seen 'em. They're real cute younkers. Tarnation, we jest can't do this and you're being damned unfair asking us to.'

'Who said that?' Mort said.

His fierce stare searched the morose-looking bunch. The orange-yellow light of the sun setting over the distant piney hills shone directly on to his face. Now obviously frustrated by this unusual resistance to his plans he said,

'The hell's the matter with you all? We're doing right here. Goddamnit, I don't know why I'm putting up with this!'

Jim saw his opportunity. 'I'll tell you why, because you know in your own gut this ain't right.' He pulled at the brim of his dusty Stetson. 'Dammit, Mort, if we go any further with this we'll be in even bigger trouble than we are now. I keep telling you things aren't like they used to be. Range justice is dead. Get it through that head of yours or you'll get us all hung, y'hear? We're ridin'. If Sheriff Dixon's a mind, he can do the checkin'.' But he knew his words were falling on deaf ears.

Abruptly, Mort turned his horse and pointed it south. Then stared hard at his lined-up crew.

'We've wasted enough time here,' he barked. 'We're gittin', y'hear?' After one more glare he dug in his spurs and headed south.

The Slash B hands hesitated, then Bowdy Gleason shrugged and looked around at the crew as if to say, *Well, it's not as though we ain't done this before, huh, boys?*

They urged their mounts after Mort.

But Jim hung back, indecision plaguing him. For one thing, to leave Cadman's body lying there and open to being savaged and eaten by hungry animals stuck in his craw. But with Mort in his present murderous mood, that was how it would have to be. What was needed now was that he should do his utmost to save Cadman's wife and her children.

With Mort in this mood, it wasn't going to be easy.

CHAPTER FIVE

Near an hour later, and along with the rest of the Slash B riders, Jim hauled rein on the edge of the grove of cottonwoods and willows that grew by Newton Creek. The brook babbled soothingly in the silver darkness beyond where they were.

It had been a long day and Jim watched the boys climb down, with tired resignation, to work the kinks out of their legs and bodies.

Jim stared at the cabin, standing peaceful in the moonlight and situated on a gentle rise of ground a hundred yards back from the murmuring creek No lamplight shone through the kinks in the shuttered windows. Indeed, there appeared to be no sign of life at all. Jim began to wonder, even hopefully, whether Cadman's woman had been warned of their coming and had moved out Even so, he thought, burning the cabin was a senseless thing to do. He stared at Mort.

'There ain't no point to this,' he said.

He saw fury rise once more in Mort's square features as, with an angry growl, he pulled his Smith & Wesson American six-shot and lined it up.

'Damn you, Jim,' he said, 'you've got ten seconds to make your mind up which side you're on here. This time I ain't bluffin'.'

Jim stared at the menacing dark round bore, aimed at his heart. There was something mighty wrong here, he decided. This man pointing that lethal weapon had been his friend for nigh on twenty-five years. Had his mind really gone? Jim fought to calm himself.

'Mort,' he said quietly, 'put the gun away; we need to talk this out.'

Mort tensed and blinked. Jim watched slight bewilderment come to his friend. After moments Mort looked down at the weapon in his hand. He appeared surprised to see the pistol nestling there. Indeed, he inspected it as if now puzzled by its presence in his hand. After some moments he shook his head in a perplexed way and slowly holstered the weapon in its customary cross-draw position. Then, as if he was a sulky child who'd had his toys taken away from him he said,

'Why are you goin' agin me, Jim? Damn you, you're tryin' me real bad these days, contradicting me all the time. Just what's gotten into you? I allus considered you to be the one man I could depend on.'

'And you can,' Jim said, 'but I got to repeat: you're not yourself these days; you've got to get help.' He watched his friend's red face swell once more with anger.

'Damn you, there you go agin! Jim, there ain't nothin' wrong with me, I tell you. It's you, you're losing your nerve.' He paused as if the next words had suddenly dawned on him. 'Yeah, dammit, that's it, your nerve's, gone. Jim, this has got to be done. Get it through your head.'

Jim now knew there was no talking to the man. He turned and looked at the Cadman homestead. It was a well-built five-roomed structure made from caulked pine boles. It was capped with a shingle roof. Cadman and his wife must have put a hell of a lot of sweated labour into this place. With one last hope of changing Mort's mind he said,

'Mort, you can't burn this woman out. She's done you no harm at all. Dammit, man, where's your compassion; you had it once. An' we gotta check if the woman and her children are still in there. Got to.'

Mort cut the night air with a dismissive hand.

'Horse dung!' he said. 'The place is in darkness. It's empty. Somebody's warned them we're coming. They've quit. That's as plain as the nose on your face.'

'It ain't plain,' Jim said, his rage suddenly rising to boiling point. 'To hell with you, I'm going to take a look.'

He climbed down off his horse and began to stride towards the dark, silent cabin. Then, causing him to falter, he heard Mort's Smith & Wesson once more issue clicks as it was being armed.

'Git back on your horse, Jim,' Mort said, taut calmness in his voice. 'Don't force my hand.'

'Go to hell, I tell you!'

His backbone tingling with now genuine fear Jim strode on, but his mind was in turmoil. He had never known Mort to be like this. He had to get his friend medical attention; the man had gone plumb crazy.

'I will kill you' Mort shouted.

'Then do it and be damned!' Jim said.

Mort gave out a strangled cry. 'Jim! I mean it!'

But Jim kept walking. He heard the clatter of hoofs

31

behind him. He turned, to see Mort riding hard towards him, Smith & Wesson raised, ready to strike. Alarm rising in him, he moved as quickly as he could, but he knew he was too late. Mort's weapon was already swinging down in a blue-black arc. It hit him across the left side of his head. Pain speared through him and blackness engulfed him.

Jim became aware of the raging thump of pain in his head and then the grassy ground beneath him, its rich earthy smell filling his nostrils. Next he became conscious of intense heat. It felt as though it was burning the skin off his back and singeing his hair. Further away, bright orange-yellow light illuminated the whole area now and the roar of burning timber raged in his ears. By God, he'd done it!

Jim fought his way out of his dazed condition. He struggled to his feet and shook his head in an attempt to clear his thinking. After moments, recollection came: Mort, riding down on him, six-gun raised and ready to strike, then the blow to his head and then intense blackness.

Now came the squeaking grind of collapsing wood that brought him to full alertness. He looked up. Cadman's neat homestead was a raging inferno. Flames were leaping skywards amid a multitude of vivid, dancing sparks. Hot air scorched his face and he staggered back, holding up his arms in an attempt to protect his face from the fierce invasion of heat. Then alarm rushed through him as the next thought hit him. *The Cadman woman and her children . . . were they in there?*

As if to answer the unthinkable he saw Jane Cadman staggering out of the flames, only to collapse, screaming and burning, on to the boards of the blazing stoop. Even more horrendous, her children, one grasped on each side of her but ablaze and obviously dead, were being pulled down with her.

He reacted instinctively. Ignoring the heat he lunged forward. If he could get to the woman there might be a chance he could save her. But he hadn't gone four paces before he felt a powerful hand grip the top of his shirt and jerk him back.

He twisted round and glared.

'What the hell?'

It was Mort holding him. Disbelief was stamped into every line of his friend's craggy features.

'Jim, they're done for,' he said. 'Get the hell back before *you* fry.'

'And you've done it, by God!' Jim said.

He tore himself out of Mort's grip and once more made toward the blaze, holding his hands in front of his face in an attempt to shield it from the extreme heat. But it was too much and he staggered back to watch, helplessly, as the raging inferno swallowed up Jane Cadman and her children.

Now, feeling sick, he turned away and fell to his knees. Out of sheer frustration he savagely began to beat the ground with his fists, but knowing that nothing would relieve the revulsion he held for his friend right now. Then, after what seemed an age and fully calm, he stared up at Mort.

'Happy now?' he said.

To his surprise he saw that shock was registered in Mort's intense blue eyes, aand that it was also deep enough to be etched into his now unusually pale face. Also, Mort was shaking his head as if he, too, was staggered by the appalling consequences of what had been done here. After more moments, made pregnant with his obvious remorse, he said,

'As God's my judge, Jim, I didn't want this to happen.'

Rage burst through Jim like a Missouri flood.

'Damn you!' he said, 'I wanted to go in there an' check but you beat the shit outa me to prevent me.'

Mort held out his hands imploringly; he appeared to be almost crying

'Jim,' he said, 'I thought they'd be gone. Honest to God I did!'

Jim roared, 'You never tried to find out, damn you!'

Then he grasped his head. Forgotten in the awfulness of the recent events, he was now aware of the throbbing, acute pain there. Cursing – he was too angry to groan – he dabbed the still freely bleeding wound while he tried to make sense of this senseless situation. What had happened to his friend of twenty-five years? At one time – and not that long ago – Mort had been the most considerate of men and could be kind to a fault, if the mood took him. Jim shook his head. He'd thought he knew the man, inside as well as out. Dammit, they'd been through hell together. Why, one time Mort had even saved his life.

He fought down his rage and waited until he was calm enough to speak. Then he said,

'You know there will be hell to pay for this.'

Mort's look was now sullen. He sliced the air with a calloused right hand.

'I'll deal with it,' he said. Then he stared at the bloody cloth Jim now held to his skull and made a weak gesture. 'Sorry about your head.'

Jim shook his head and waved a dismissive hand before

he said,

'Mort, I'll say it again: you're not a well man. You've got to see a doctor.' He tapped his aching head. 'Things ain't right in there, you got to know that.'

From an expression of deep remorse, Mort's face once more flared into raging anger.

'There's nothing wrong with me, y'hear?' He shook a stubby finger; his stare behind the gesture looked like two bullet heads. 'It's you need seein' to,' he said. 'Yeah . . . it's you who needs to see the sawbones – about your nerves. Man, this had to be done and you know it. This never troubled you at one time.'

Jim shook his head in despair. 'Mort, the old days are done. This is murder and you know it.'

He turned and went to his horse, which was cropping the sparse grass under the blaze-illuminated trees. But before he could mount Mort was beside him and grabbing his arm.

'Why d'you keep making out I'm crazy?'

'Because you are,' Jim said. 'And not only me has noticed; the men have caught on to the fact, too.'

Mort slowly released his grip. Jim saw disbelief was now registered in every hollow of his friend's craggy face.

After moments of what Jim construed to be deliberation, Mort's face brightened and he adopted a sly look.

'I've got it now; you're lying.' He wagged a finger. 'Yeah, that's it you're lying because you want to get me in some loony house so you can get your hands on the ranch. That's it, ain't it? Go on, say I'm wrong.'

'You're wrong,' Jim said.

'Pah! You can't even lie good.' Mort turned to the cowhands standing under the trees, their drawn faces

35

illuminated by the raging fire. 'You been listenin'? Is that what you think . . . that I'm crazy?' He glared. 'Come on, damn you! Say it if you think it.'

Most of the riders gave him morose stares and then studied the dark trees and black night above the raging fire, clearly not wanting to comment. Mort glared.

'What's the matter with you? Ain't you got the guts to say it?'

Frank Lawson lifted his head and met Mort's stare head on. He had been with Slash B for ten years.

'I got the guts, Mr Basset,' he said quietly. 'It's like Jim said, you ain't yourself these days – not since what happened to your family.'

Jim tensed. He expected to see Mort's Smith & Wesson being drawn and lined up on Frank Lawson. He loosened his own Colt in readiness to counter the possibility. However, slowly the anger in Mort's face drained as he said,

'Well, at least you got the guts to come out and say it, Frank, and I can only thank you for that.'

He turned. Jim met his stare. 'Give ol' Frank here a fortnight's extra pay for his honesty, Jim, will yah?'

Jim took his hand away from his Colt. He wanted to shake his head in dismay, but didn't. For this was how his old friend was these days – unpredictable. Instead, he said,

'I'll see to it.'

He mounted his horse, pulled it around and waited for the rest of the crew to climb into saddles. Then they silently rode out. Soon deep darkness swallowed them up.

CHAPTER SIX

Three hours back

The crack of a rifle shot.

Luke Freeman, John Cadman's friend from the age of ten, and also his neighbour and related – his wife being the sister of John's wife – perked up and watched as the eight riders about a mile ahead of him moved out towards the sound.

Luke narrowed his calm grey eyes. That shot could mean anything. Maybe somebody was in trouble, perhaps suffering a broken a leg, and had fired their long gun in the hope of attracting attention.

That did happen from time to time.

However, shots, particularly in this lonely part of the basin, could mean other more dangerous things, despite the politicians claiming that illegal shootings and the crude range justice that had been practised by the ranchers and not all that long ago, were now at an end in Wild Horse Basin.

Luke guided his big draught horse down the rock-and-tree-strewn slope of the ridge from which he had been scanning the landscape. Soon he gained level ground.

Riding easier now, he determined that the sound of the shot had come from the arroyo that cut a deep gash across the east section of the broad basin.

He compressed lean lips as he became acutely aware of the tingling excitement, the distinct prickle of fear, that now caused his red blood to surge through him. Most certainly, he decided, caution would be needed here.

Reaching the cover of the trees a hundred or so yards from the arroyo's rim, he peered through the screen of aspen and cottonwoods. Shock jarred through his veins like icy melt water. Mort Basset and seven members of his crew had got John surrounded. A couple of bruised and blood-smeared cowpunchers were firmly holding him on his big Morgan horse. John seemed to have been battered, too. But most gut-wrenching of all, John had a noose around his neck, the long tail of which had been thrown over a cottonwood bough and secured near the base of the trunk.

Instinctively, Luke reached for his well-used Springfield rifle, the one he'd carried to good effect throughout the Civil War. It was cased in the saddle holster by his right knee, but was now used only to shoot game should the chance arise to put meat on the table. Then he paused and lowered his hand. What good was a single-shot rifle against the repeating Winchesters he knew the majority of cowmen carried these days? On top of that, there were eight men gathered around John. It would be crazy even to attempt anything so stupid. And, further hindering that reaction, what about his now deep Christian beliefs? In particular the commandment, *Thou shalt not kill?* Indeed, he had given up killing men years ago because of his conversion.

38

However, agitated almost beyond belief now, Luke continued to stare. Basset. The very sight of the man caused the cold hand of fear to clamp his gut, for it was claimed that Basset was doing crazy things these days, ever since the Sioux had murdered his wife and two girls, and rustlers, not two months later, killed his three boys as they drove a herd of cattle to Wichita.

Terrible tragedies for a man to endure, Luke decided. But, and this was the disturbing thing, it was rumoured that Mort Basset had become severely deranged by those two awful happenings and, for some strange reason, was now openly blaming the farmers for the distress he was suffering.

Luke realized a cold sweat had now formed beads on his brow. If these rumours were true then John was in mortal danger here. Dear God, what was he to do? If he rode into what was going on across there he too would surely be killed. God of love, he had a wife and three children to look out for. Further, he would also have John's wife and two children to take care of should the worst happen here. For before they even headed West, John and he had made a pact: that should misfortune befall either one of them, the survivor would undertake the responsibility of looking after the other fellow's wife and children. Indeed, it had been a solemn pledge made on the Holy Bible before both gathered families.

He scanned the grim-looking bunch of men who were standing around John. His gaze settled on Jim Alston, the Slash B foreman. It was known that Alston was a reasonable man and a close friend of Basset. Surely he must have some influence over the Slash B owner? Maybe if he rode in and appealed to Alston, he would—

A roar of anger, interrupting his thoughts, came from the direction of the Slash B. He swung his gaze away from Alston and saw that Basset, red of face, was now standing up in his stirrups, shaking his fist and shouting at John.

'Damn you, Cadman, for the devil you are!'

Then the crazed man swung his quirt across the rump of John's big Morgan horse and shouted, 'Git, damn you, hoss, git!'

The large startled animal took off, leaving – Oh! God in heaven! – John swinging on the end of the rope. Immediately despair enveloped Luke like a huge black cloud. Then misery swung back to hope as he saw that Jim Alston, the tall Slash B foreman, was spurring forward.

On reaching John, Jim Alston slashed the rope apart with his big Bowie knife, then dismounted and ran to where John had fallen into the dust.

Reaching him Alston, after moments stared up at the Slash B men who were gathered around, sitting their horses and viewing the scene with apparent callous indifference. Alston was shaking his head. His lean face was set in a grim mask. It did not take much imagination on Luke's part to work out what that headshake meant: John was dead.

Luke felt something like a lead weight hit the bottom of his stomach. But he did not have time to dwell on that awful conclusion, for angry words were being exchanged across there. Then, abruptly and clearly in a vile temper, red-faced Basset turned his horse and spurred toward the south. After only momentary hesitation the Slash B hands urged their mounts and followed him. Jim Alston was the only man hesitating. Then he, too, after a sad shake of his head, joined them.

South? Luke felt the nerves in his gut scramble. John's cabin was to the south. Jane and her children – Janice and Mary – would be in there waiting for John to come home. Further agitation grabbed at Luke as his next thought hit him. Slash B would not – surely *could* not – burn them out? But after this horror, and Basset acting so crazy, Luke decided anything was possible, and such things had been common practice in the basin not so long ago. Range justice they called it.

Luke prepared to dig in heels and follow them; then he refrained. What was he doing? First he must check if John was really dead.

He found that his brother-in-law was dead. He stared into John's grey, dead eyes. It was an agonizing decision he had to make now, but the burying of John would have to wait, no matter what pain that decision caused him.

Closing down on his terrible grief and frustration he turned his Morgan horse after Basset and his crew. It would be the equivalent of a snail chasing a greyhound, he knew. However, he would do it. But what he would do when he got to where they were going, only God knew that.

CHAPTER SEVEN

Twilight was long gone by the time Luke got close to Newton Creek. An almost full moon and a myriad of brilliant stars now silvered the night sky. It would have been a truly wondrous sight had it not been for the orange-yellow flare he could see illuminating the sky beyond the craggy, moon-silvered ridge a mile and a half ahead of him. Raw anxiety twisted his gut into a knot. That blaze could only mean one thing. John's homestead was ablaze. He urged his near-exhausted horse into giving him one last burst of speed.

Fifty yards below the crest of the hill overlooking John's cabin he eased back on the rein and climbed down. He tethered the heavily breathing and sweating beast behind a thick clump of mesquite and scrambled to the brow of the ridge. He peered down.

Despite expecting the sight, what he saw still shocked him to the core of his being. John's house was a roaring inferno and Jim Alston, despite the heat that the fire must be pushing out, was running towards it. Even more strange, mounted Mort Basset was chasing Alston, his pistol raised ready to strike down, which he did when he got close enough to the Slash B foreman.

Amazed, Luke watched Alston stagger under the blow, his tall hat flying off his head, before he sprawled into the dirt, clearly unconscious. Then, causing Luke even more concern, came the harsh sound of rending timber. He watched, his gut clenching up in anguish, as the roof of the homestead caved in amid showers of sparks and roaring flames. But most terrible of all, the blazing form of Jane, her two clearly dead children clasped one each side of her, came staggering out of those raging flames to stand screaming in her agony on the burning stoop. Even more ghastly, without warning the shingle roof suddenly collapsed down upon Jane and the children and they disappeared, engulfed by that raging horror. Then within the compass of Luke's stunned gaze, Basset dismounted and dragged Jim Alston away from the fire's fury.

Alston appeared to be regaining consciousness. When the man realized what was happening he struggled to his feet and angrily ripped himself out of Basset's grasp to once more struggle toward the furnace heat of the blazing cabin, as if he was blind to the fact that there was no longer anything he could do there.

Luke gripped hard on his Springfield rifle until his knuckles showed white. God, how he wanted to charge down there and kill Basset with a bullet between the eyes. But then the mind's-eye picture of Maureen, his wife, and the faces of his three children came to him and he knew then he could not do it despite the terrible things that had happened here. The needs of his family must come first, last and foremost. However, the frustration he felt was hardly bearable. At one time he had been a formidable fighting man with a deadly draw. Then Maureen came into his life from God knew where. He didn't ask; all persons have history in this wild territory, and it was not always good to enquire.

In any case, by then he was a man deeply in love for the first time in his life, so her past did not matter a damn to him. He just wanted her love, the feel of her in his arms, her perfume in his nostrils, the warm essence of her. However, the first shock came when he proposed. Those intense blue eyes of hers studied him. Then she declared, with a lift of her pretty chin, that before she could even think of marrying him he would have to shed his guns and turn to the Lord their God. If he failed to do so then there would be no point in continuing their relationship.

The declaration stunned him. He'd never heard the like of it before. Surely, a woman must follow the path her man chose once the marriage knot was tied? That was how it was and how it had always been, in his experience anyway.

Nevertheless, he was soon to discover that some women, Maureen in particular, had this bar of steel running right through them when circumstances required it. And it seemed that she had this ability to subtly, but relentlessly chew away at a man's will until she got what she wanted.

Oh, he'd fought, wriggled, stamped, protested. But in truth he had been trying to find a new path to tread after all the killing he had personally done and terrible things he had witnessed being done during the Civil War. For at one time, he'd had a three-times-on-Sunday Christian upbringing and had been a devout Christian until he had been called to serve in the terrible conflict on the Union side. So he found, when he finally made the transition, that on Maureen's implacable insistence he did not find it too difficult to do, even though on leaving the army, he had thought guns were the only means of solving problems in this wild country.

Luke's attention was diverted again. They were arguing down there. Was it about how to hide or deny this ghastly atrocity? For, apart from Alston, that's what they would be doing, he fervently believed. Indeed, he had no doubts they would head straight back to Slash B. Most certainly they would not head for town. When the time came to answer for this crime they would deny all knowledge of what had happened here. Basset would see to that.

Luke tensed. They were moving now. He watched them turn their horses and ride off into the night. It was then that he cried, long and bitterly and prayed for the souls of Jane and the children, even though he already knew they would find peace and eternal life in the arms of their Lord.

Only God knew how his wife Maureen would react to the terrible news he would bring – and the children for that matter. However, right now, there was the matter of Jane's and the children's ashes, as well as John's body sprawled on the ground back on South Range. When he could he must recover those remains, take them into Broken Mesa and alert the law as to what had been done here.

Resolved, he approached the blazing ruin, only to be driven back by the intense heat. On second thoughts he now considered – was it really such a good idea to disturb Jane's and the children's ashes and collect John? Would it not be better to leave what remains there were for Sheriff Talbot Dixon to witness? Yes. Come tomorrow he would ride into Broken Mesa and inform the lawman of the lynching of John and the ghastly burning of Jane and her children. Then he would lead the sheriff to where he could witness the results of Basset and his men's evil, for he was sure that Basset and his crew would want to keep these terrible crimes quiet. What else would such evil murderers do?

Mid-afternoon the following day he rode into Broken Mesa only to learn that Mort Basset had not tried to hide anything. In fact, he had done the opposite. The town's citizenry were full of the story. Luke soon gathered that Basset and his men had ridden straight into town from Newton Creek, changed their worn-out horses at Gibson's livery stables and then ridden on to rouse Sheriff Talbot Dixon out of his bed with the sole purpose of reporting the killings.

After that, less than an hour later, Slash B had ridden out as part of Sheriff Dixon's posse, their aim apparently being to show the lawman exactly where John's body was, and also the remains of Jane and the children. No doubt they would tell a string of lies in the process.

Luke then learned, to his huge surprise, that Dixon's posse had returned an hour before noon this very day with John's body on the back of the spare horse the posse had taken for that purpose. Moreover, Jane's and the children's remains were reported to be in a doeskin bag tied securely to Sheriff Dixon's saddle horn. All were duly dropped off at Jacob Farley's funeral parlour, Jacob being the town's carpenter and undertaker. Then, and this was like an arrow to the heart, Dixon had allowed Basset and his men to ride home on the promise that, after food and sleep, they would return to town the following day.

That, in Luke's thinking, was near inexplicable. At the very least Basset should have been held and jailed. But Luke also knew that Basset had considerable influence in Wild Horse Basin, even to the point that, at one time, Basset had thought of standing for governor until the trauma of losing his family to outlaws and Sioux Indians sent him near crazy and killed any ambitions he had in that direction stone dead.

Nevertheless, Basset was still a big man hereabouts, Luke knew, particularly among the large ranching community. Despite that, Luke decided there was still hope. Sheriff Talbot Dixon had come to this territory with a strong reputation for upholding the law and letting nothing stand in his way in the execution of it. Yet Dixon had allowed Basset and the Slash B crew to return to the ranch on the promise that they would return on the morrow

Digesting that, Luke narrowed his eyes and clamped together his lean lips. That fact left a whisper of doubt, so what tomorrow would bring would be interesting, to say the least.

CHAPTER EIGHT

It was two hours into full dark when Luke arrived back at his homestead by Byron Creek. The three children, Betty, six, Lucy, four, and James, three, were in bed, as they rightly should be at this hour.

On his return last night he had acquainted his wife Maureen with the news of John's death and of the other horrors he had witnessed.

As he told it, he watched her heart-shaped face pale. However, when she appeared to have absorbed the dreadful news a cold, intense light began to grow in her blue eyes. It was a look he had never seen before. He had expected her to nearly disintegrate with the horror of the news but she'd remained rigidly still and silent, her face set into a stiff mask. Then, after a minute or so, when she appeared to have resolved what she was thinking over in her mind, she said,

'I need to go out for a while, husband. Don't follow me.'

Luke felt alarm clench his stomach. 'You ain't goin' to . . .'

'Take my life?' She smiled, but it was a wan, tired smile.

'That would go against the Lord's teachings, as well you know, Luke Freeman.' Then she went through the door, closing it softly behind her.

Anxious, he watched her through the one glazed window as she stood in the little garden of flowers she'd made and tended with such loving care ever since they arrived here. She stared up at the moon and the star-filled sky, as she always did when she wanted to commune with the Lord their God. As he watched thoughts crept into his mind regarding how things stood with *him* after the terrible things that had occurred. Indeed, the need for revenge now clawed at his innards like some invasive, burrowing critter.

He should start wearing his six-gun again. However, he had made a promise to Maureen way back not to wear his Colt ever again or to commit violent acts, when she insisted he become, like her, a committed Christian before she would marry him. But right now, how could he *not* do that manly thing if justice was not otherwise to be fully served on those Slash B killers?

The constraint angered him, made him feel like a cringing coward. Nevertheless, he had made that pledge and he would not renege on it. He had no choice.

When Maureen had finished in the garden some hours later she came to bed. Though he was awake he did not speak, nor did he mention his recent thoughts about taking up arms again in the hope that she might release him from his oath. His failure to discuss those thoughts troubled him now, for they had always been so honest with each other. Now, because he had failed to do that, the whole thing was pressing on his mind like a ton weight, and sleep was a long time coming.

*

Maureen and the children were still fast asleep when he left to go to Broken Mesa. Though he arrived in the town around eleven o'clock it was an hour after noon before the bunch of Slash B riders, headed by Mort Basset, gathered before Broken Mesa's red-brick law office and jail.

Luke watched, bleak-eyed, as a dour-looking Sheriff Talbot Dixon and one of his three deputies, George Smith by name, came out of the office to stand grim-faced on the dusty boardwalk. Dixon's right hand was resting on the butt of his Colt. He ranged his steel-grey gaze across the row of Slash B riders before he settled it on Basset.

'I want no trouble, Mort,' he said quietly.

'You won't get it,' Basset said. 'This matter will be cleared up, satisfactory to all.'

'I doubt that,' Dixon said.

Clearly not liking the reply Basset glared at Dixon before he turned to the crowd that was now nearly blocking Main Street.

'I guess you've all heard about the Cadman business?' he shouted.

The press of people moved restlessly; a few answered 'Yes', some even nodded and said, 'Sure'.

'Well, as God's my judge,' Mort went on, 'I did not want this to happen, but Cadman forced it on me with his downright thievery.'

Full of rage Luke wanted to yell 'Liar', but held his peace. Basset paused and eased himself to a better position in the saddle before he continued.

'However, I will pay all funeral expenses so that the

Cadman family can be decently buried in the large churchyard we now have and for which, I might add, I gave a large contribution to help in its construction.'

More anger churned in Luke's stomach. Clever. The recently built place of worship stood half a mile north of town. It was the place where the new settlers in the basin, the farmers, the businessmen, the railwaymen, the retailers and even some saddle hands, gathered every Sunday to sing hymns, say prayers and listen to the thunderous hellfire and damnation sermons preached by the fearsomely frowning Pastor Hannibal Griffiths. Standing at the front of the crowd, Luke strived to subdue his anger. It would serve no purpose to vent his rage at the moment. Instead he said,

'The buryin'll be my responsibility, Basset.'

The large gathering went tomb quiet and the Slash B owner glared down.

'Just who in hell be *you*, mister?' he demanded.

Jim Alston leaned over and said, 'Luke Freeman; Cadman's neighbour.'

'And friend,' Luke added.

'Friend, uh?' Basset sneered. He turned to the men behind him, and guffawed. 'Well, God a' mighty, boys, did Mr Cadman have *friends*?' He waved an arm as if inviting the boys to join in. Some did, others just stared with passive indifference.

Clearly not getting all the reaction he was looking for Basset turned his stare upon Luke again, all humour gone now.

'Well, hell, if you want them remains, take them and welcome. For, sure as ever will be, Cadman was just a nogood thieving son of a bitch and deserved all he got.'

Luke's anger roared through him like a rampant prairie fire. The urge to run forward and drag that arrogant devil out of his saddle and beat him to a pulp was now a nearly overwhelming requirement. With a huge effort of will he held down his rage and said,

'Thief? What you talking about, Basset?'

The Slash B owner's eyes widened, as if in mock surprise.

'You telling me you don't know? Him bein' your great friend, an' all?'

Luke nodded, his stare implacable. 'I am.'

Basset rocked moodily in the saddle, again all mirth gone.

'He killed a prime beeve of mine for meat. Caught him red-handed, butchering it.'

'You're lying,' Luke said. 'John Cadman never stole a thing in his life. There's got to be another reason.'

Basset's square face flushed with sudden rage. After some moments, he said,

'Mister, I'll overlook the accusation of lying for now. I appreciate you are distraught. But don't make a habit of it, y'hear me? Or things'll be different.' He turned to Sheriff Dixon. 'Tell him what you saw out there on South Range, Talbot.'

Though clearly uneasy, Dixon said, 'It appeared to be that way, Freeman. The beast was in an arroyo, shot through the head. All the Slash B men said they heard the shot that killed the beeve, and when they got to the arroyo edge there was Cadman, cutting off a haunch. The boys also reported his rifle was leaning against a rock close by and was still warm to the touch. It sure looked that way when I viewed the site, though by then the rifle was cold, of course.'

Luke said, 'I still don't believe it. John would not do that.'

Dixon shrugged and said, 'You have that choice, but that's how I saw it, so did the posse of people who came out with me from town, all of whom I believe are neutral, with no axe to grind.'

'Did you go down there?' Luke asked. 'Look it over?'

'No, there seemed little point,' Dixon replied. 'What happened was plain to see from the top of the arroyo.'

Luke found he was still having difficulty holding down his temper. Though he was staring at Dixon, he waved an accusing finger in Basset's direction.

'Well hear this, lawman: that man lynched John. *Lynched* him, y'hear?' Luke straightened his six-foot, powerful frame and scowled. 'I was given to understand hanging a man without trial was now illegal in this territory.'

Calmly, Dixon nodded. 'And so it is,' he said. 'How the incident will be punished will be decided at the trial.'

Luke glared. 'Incident? You got the gall to call the burning of a man's innocent wife and children an *incident?*'

Dixon's grey look took on a hard edge. 'That, too, will be dealt with, Freeman. You have my word.'

Though not satisfied with the reply, Luke said, 'About the remains. . . .'

Dixon turned to the Slash B owner. 'Well? How about them?'

Mort waved an indifferent hand. 'Hell, if he wants them let him take 'em. It'll sure as hell save me money.'

Dixon nodded and turned. Luke met his stare.

'They're over at Jacob Farley's place,' Dixon said. 'Pick them up when you're ready.'

'I'm ready,' Luke said. 'Meantime, what happens to Basset and his men? You jailing them?'

Dixon shook his head. 'Not all,' he said, 'Basset will be jailed until trial time, of course, but—'

Basset's angry growl interrupted, 'The hell are you saying here, Dixon?'

The lawman stared at him with bleak grey eyes.

'I think you heard; you stay here but your men are free to return to Slash B. However, they will be put on their honour to make themselves available for trial when the time comes.'

'They have no honour,' Luke said, bitterly.

Eight pairs of hostile eyes glared down at him from atop their horses, and Basset said,

'By, God, mister, you'd better watch your tongue from hereon. We ain't used to bein' talked to like that, especially by some goddamned granger.'

'That's enough!' Dixon said, and as smooth as quicksilver he drew his Colt and aimed at Slash B owner's midriff. 'Climb down, Mort.'

Basset stayed in the saddle, his stare the colour of blue ice.

'You know what you're saying here, Dixon? You know what I mean to this basin . . . what I've done?'

'I know what you *have* been, but aren't any longer,' Dixon said. He turned to Deputy Smith. 'Take his weapon, George, and drag him off his horse if he don't climb down peaceably.'

The deputy nodded, grinned. 'Will do.' He stepped down from the boardwalk into the street dust. He took two paces, then he reached up and yanked Basset's six-gun out of its worn holster.

Basset didn't resist, but Luke saw evil in the Slash B owner's stare as he levelled it on Dixon. Then he said, his voice held low and confidential,

'Talbot, you are making a big mistake here, you realize that? I could bury you.' Then he leaned back in the saddle and added, 'However, if you're reasonable an' let me ride home with my men I could make things mighty easy for you come next election time, an' I guarantee I'll return with my men when trial time comes.'

'Don't threaten me, Basset, and don't try to bribe me,' Dixon said. He turned to Jim Alston, seated close by on his horse next to Basset. 'Take your men back to the ranch, Alston; you'll be called when needed.'

Luke watched the Slash B foreman stiffen and flick his gaze across to Basset, as if asking the silent question with raised eyebrows: *do we stay or go?*

'Do as he says, Jim,' Basset said. Then, mean-eyed, he eased down off his horse and climbed the two steps to the boardwalk. The unblinking black bore of Dixon's pointed Colt followed him all the way. Then standing close to the lawman the Slash B owner turned and said,

'Still time to change your mind on this.'

The lawman's grey-eyed stare bored into Basset's features.

'Don't ever try to bribe or threaten me again, Basset,' he said. He then prodded the Slash B owner in the ribs with his Colt. 'Now, get inside.'

Basset spread a cold grin across his ragged face, shrugged and turned to Jim Alston.

'Seems to me this man don't know which side his bread's

buttered, Jim,' he said, 'so take the boys and yourself home.'

Alston nodded. 'As you say,' he said and then added, as if it was an afterthought, 'I'll arrange to have Dolly Grover bring over your vittles. It'll be better than county slop, I warrant.'

Mort nodded. 'You never let me down, old friend,' he said. Then he stared at Dixon. 'Lead on, lawman; I'll be right behind you. Haw, haw, haw!'

Dixon appeared to hold no appreciation of Basset's warped humour.

'Joker too, huh?' he said. 'Git in there, damn you!'

Basset's grin stayed. 'Joker? Better believe it, friend,' he said, but with no humour in his voice. He headed into the office, all the time prompted by the hard jab of Dixon's six-gun into his kidney region.

CHAPTER NINE

Three weeks later, the last day of the trial, Luke and Maureen along with their three children, sat at the back of the packed courtroom, as they had done during the whole proceedings. Throughout Luke had observed that Basset was prepared and had come out fighting whenever he was called to the dock.

The rancher maintained he did right in hanging John. However, he was at pains to add that he and his men bitterly regretted the deaths of the woman and her children; they would have to live with that regret for the rest of their lives.

On that basis defence counsel – slick-talking Eastern lawyers shipped in by Basset – submitted in their summing up that indeed the burning of Jane and her children had been a terrible tragedy, but an accident, a sad misfortune; one that as the accused had already stated, would be on their consciences until the day they died.

However, on the street at each day's end Luke found that more than a few town folk, when discussing the subject, fiercely brought that argument into question.

Some declared that Mort Basset did not know the

meaning of regret, let alone be able to experience it. Even so, it also became clear that, despite the local hostility, Mort Basset was still a power in the basin and had more than a few influential friends in the county and beyond. And, not hindering matters, Basset was also the head of the county cattleman's association and a hefty contributor to the taxman's purse. In a lot of cowmen's minds and those of some in the county's governing body, these facts all added up to an acquittal.

Now, on this last day, with a searching gaze Luke stared around him to see the eager anticipation on the faces of the people filling the courtroom. With defence and prosecuting counsels' closing speeches now done, the buzz of talk welled up and then quietened down when Judge Neilson, the county's resident justice, loudly cleared his throat in preparation for summing up. Then he began, with all due gravity.

'Members of the jury, this is a sad and, in some ways a painful duty I have now to perform, but one that has to be judged on the evidence laid before this court.' He paused to take a deep, asthmatic breath before continuing.

'And deplorable though the hanging of John Cadman was, it must be viewed as justified in the face of the evidence put before us. However, regarding the deaths of Cadman's wife and children . . . well, I feel bound to go along with defence counsel's eminently persuasive plea that it was, though a regrettable and intensely heart-rending affair, an *accident*: a case of the man's family being in the wrong place at the wrong time.'

Luke wanted to jump up and roar his disagreement. However, hard as it was to hold back from denouncing this farce, he held his peace and Judge Neilson droned on for another five minutes before he invited the jury to retire and consider its verdict. They did not take long.

Ten minutes later the jury filed back in.

Luke felt Maureen become tense beside him; saw her clasp her hands tightly together in her lap until they showed stark white. She 'shushed' the children, who were becoming restless, then she and Luke waited.

Once more Judge Neilson cleared his throat and looked owlishly over the top of his spectacles before speaking.

'Gentlemen of the jury,' he said, 'how find you?' Tall and solemn-faced the foreman stood and announced, gravely,

'Not guilty of all charges, your honour.'

Gasps of disbelief rippled throughout the full courtroom, accompanied by hefty whoops and cheers from the large gathering of cattlemen.

Scowling across the crowded assembly Judge Neilson banged down his gavel several times.

'Silence!'

The uproar in the courtroom rumbled down to quiescence and Judge Neilson glared around the sweaty crowd that was now beginning to give forth, because of the heat, the stench of unwashed bodies, horse sweat and cow dung, mingled with the occasional whiff of cologne or lavender water from the ladies.

'Better,' Neilson said, with a further glower. 'Now, like it or not, this is the decision of twelve good men and true and this court upholds that decision.' The judge paused before adding, 'However, I will take this opportunity to make it known that times are changing here in Wild Horse Basin. Should any rancher or sodbuster, or anybody else think of taking the law into their own hands in future, this court will come down on them with all the power at its command.' Then he stared directly at Mort Basset and concluded, 'No matter who is in the dock.'

Luke saw Basset flush an angry red, but the man remained silent. But raw cynicism filled Luke. Neilson. What a hypocrite! For it was already strongly rumoured in town that he – as well as a large number of those supposed twelve good men and true – had taken hefty bribes to make sure a verdict favourable to Slash B was brought in. However, as was also well known, it was another matter to prove those rumours.

With Maureen and the children, he shuffled out of the courtroom along with the rest of the vocal crowd, who were already fiercely debating the rights and wrongs of the jury's decision as they walked out on to Broad Street and into Broken Mesa's blazing early-afternoon heat. However, Maureen, though listening, remained silent by his side, her face expressionless.

Not to disturb her in her silence he ushered the children along in front because of their now constant whining and complaining. Truth was they were tired, didn't understand the gravity of what had happened. Clearly, they just wanted to go home. Well, right now, Luke brooded, that was all he wanted, having been made sick to his stomach by the travesty of justice he had been witness to this day.

They were approaching their sturdy wagon when Maureen suddenly stoppped.

'Dear Lord, forgive them, for I cannot,' she said bitterly.

Luke stared at her. Since the deaths of her sister and nieces Maureen had changed. There was a hard look in her eyes now he had never seen before. Nevertheless, he knew in his gut that due to her strong religious convictions she would eventually but certainly forgive. It would take time, maybe a long time.

In an attempt to lift his spirits Luke turned his mind to some of the reassuring moments during the trial, particularly from Sheriff Talbot Dixon. Listening to Dixon in the dock at the start of proceedings, giving what facts he knew about the tragedy, at first Luke had not been impressed. However, after Dixon had done with that business he paused and stared with those steel-grey eyes of his around the crowded courtroom. After what seemed to be a brief period of silent deliberation he took a breath and gave a forthright account of how he personally viewed the deaths of Jane and her children, and the lynching of John Cadman.

The calmly delivered pronouncements soon prompted the irate banging of Neilson's gavel and the justice's demands for Dixon to leave the dock or he would be held in contempt of court. But Dixon ignored the demands and shouted above the din of Neilson's gavel and shrill voice that the lynching of John Cadman and the burning of his family were criminal acts of the worst kind; then he turned and implored the jury – who were on oath, he fiercely reminded them – to bring in a verdict of guilty on all counts, and for the court to deliver the death sentence on Mort Basset and at least fifteen years' hard labour for the rest of his crew.

Luke remembered Neilson's gaunt, whiskered face burning red with the anger inside him.

'You far exceed your duty, Sheriff Dixon!' he thundered. Then he turned to the twelve good men and true.

'Members of the jury, you will ignore the sheriff's outburst. The *lawyers* in this court will argue the rights and wrongs of this case. Then, having heard that evidence, you will – after due deliberation, of course – deliver your verdict. Are we clear on this?'

The foreman stood and said, 'Very clear, Judge.'

Neilson then stared owlishly at Dixon. 'And are *you* hearing me on this?'

The lawman's grey eyes remained ice-cool as his gaze held Neilson's and he said, 'I stand by my words, Judge.'

Neilson's face reddened even further. 'Damn you, Talbot,' he said, 'I would hold you in contempt of court had it not been for the respect I hold for you. Nevertheless, I will require you to heed my advice in future.'

Luke recalled that Dixon had still appeared unimpressed.

'I will not retract, sir, if that's what you're looking for,' he had replied.

Luke would swear he had seen Judge Neilson quiver with anger, for it seemed that that was not the answer he had been looking for.

On the drive home – the children fast asleep in a pile of hay at the back of the wagon – Maureen remained silent, her round face flour-pale as she gazed wistfully out across the beautiful Wild Horse Basin to the majestic snow-capped mountains in the far blue distance.

Luke did not disturb her. He had always been clumsy with words where women were concerned. Most of the time he just did not know how to deal with the females of this world, but he *was* learning ... slowly. Now, as he paused on the hill overlooking their cabin, Luke felt pride. They had lived in a leaky sod hut for over a year and a half while he built, with the help of other settlers in the basin, the cabin and outbuildings. He reciprocated their help and kindness in full whenever their needs for assistance were announced.

Maureen and the other settlers' wives coped very efficiently with all the many tasks needed to keep the farms productive during the periods when the men were occupied with the building work. When Luke realized how much she had done he felt infinitely blessed to have such a capable woman by his side, particularly in this hard land.

Now arrived by the cabin he helped Maureen and the children down from the wagon, released his horse from the shafts and led it into the barn, where he tended to its needs. By the time he entered the cabin the kids had eaten a warmed-up supper of white-tail stew and were now in bed.

After he and Maureen had eaten they climbed the hill at the back of the homestead to where John, Jane and the children were buried. As he stood there bitter lines carved Luke's already grim face as he and Maureen bowed their heads.

'Dear Lord,' he said quietly, 'I guess the trial did not go the way we wanted, but You *will* punish. Of that I am sure.' By his side, Maureen cleared her throat.

'And I will add a firm amen to that, Luke Freeman,' she added huskily.

Then she went to her knees and silently prayed, while he stood to commune with the mighty Lord, who held them both in his power and who had 2,000 years ago, preached peace upon earth and love to all men, though few of His followers, as Luke had learned over the years, adhered to that impossible precept when the chips were really down. The question was, would he be able hold out? For he was a man who knew guns and how to use them and, in the past, had used them on more than one occasion.

CHAPTER TEN

It was now three weeks after the trial. Mort and Jim had watched in silent enjoyment the glorious reds and golds of a Wild Horse Basin sunset fade into night and stars and moonlight silver the vast bowl and far piny mountains beyond the hills.

Now Jim stared steadily at Mort. His great friend was contentedly smoking a long cheroot and, like him, was steadily taking in good sipping whiskey. Even more satisfying, these past three weeks Mort seemed to have become a great deal calmer, more rational. He appeared to have lost that huge rage that had been in him. It was as if, in that pinnacle of crazed madness on South Range and the shock of watching the Cadman woman and her children burn, the event had somehow jolted Mort out of his misguided need to wreak revenge; had made him see that the grangers were not responsible for the terrible things that had been done to his own family.

Jim swirled whiskey around in his shot glass. Well, for sure, he should be happy about this outcome. Or – as he really suspected – was he still striving to find grounds for believing that one tragedy had mercifully healed another?

He drew in a deep breath and stared at his friend. They were seated on cushioned wicker armchairs, enjoying the cool night air that was wafting in off the big dark range.

'I still can't git that South Range business out of my head, Mort,' he said, 'honest to God I can't.'

Mort leaned up in his wicker chair. His blue eyes were hard and searching.

'Jim, it's done.' He shook his head. 'Jees, I've never known you like this before. Get a hold of yourself, will ya? It's over and can't be changed, so live with it.'

Jim found the answer wasn't enough.

'That woman and her children . . . burning like that. Hell of a thing, Mort. Still makes me sick to my stomach just thinking about it.'

Mort thumped the arm of his chair, his face now flushing red.

'Damn you, will you quit? I agree it was bad, but it's done, over. Get that through your head, or it'll drive you crazy, y'hear?'

'That's just it, I can't git it outa my head,' Jim said. 'It's stuck there.' He scowled. 'Dammit, d'you think I ain't tried?'

Mort glared, his round face beginning to redden.

'D'you think *I* liked it – huh – huh? Do you?'

Jim stared back. 'Well, did you?'

Clearly furious now, Mort jumped up and roared, 'Damn you Jim, it was a mistake; I freely admit that and bitterly regret the deaths of the woman and her kids.' He stood, waiting for Jim's reply. When it didn't come he sat down again, sighed and said,

'Jim, old friend, you take too much to heart, allus have. For Chris' sake try to relax a little. I repeat, it's over and can't be changed. And remember, we got a spread to run. I can't do with my *jefe* mooning about the place like a cow that's lost its calf. Buckle down, it'll do you good.'

Jim swirled what was left of his whiskey in the bottom of his glass, then pursed his lips and raised his dark brows. Those were truths that had to be accepted. 'Yup, you're right there, I guess,' he said. 'Slash B must come first. We've allus agreed on that.'

'So heed it,' said Mort. He relaxed back into his cushioned chair, drew on his cheroot and blew out blue smoke. 'Now, will you be quiet and enjoy the evening?'

He paused, studied his cigar for a few seconds and then added, 'Or . . . on second thoughts, go into town, get some firewater down you, then go and find Dolly Grover. Dammit, you've got yourself taut as stretched rawhide. You need to relax and start doin' a little livin' agin.'

Jim raised thick brows. Dolly Grover. As usual, good feelings ran through him at the mention of her name. Dolly ran the thriving steakhouse on Broken Mesa's Broad Street. They'd had a loving relationship for years, though neither had wanted to be tied to the other through marriage; not yet, anyway.

He looked at his friend and formed a half-smile as he fought to forget what had happened at the Cadman place.

'You know, Mort, sometimes you talk a whole heap o' sense,' he said. Mort nodded his head vigorously.

'Damned right I do. Now go to town, see Dolly Grover, or drown those damned hang-ups you got in that head of yours with rotgut. Then get some real *sleep*. You look like hell. In fact, take a couple of days off if you feel it'll help.'

Jim drew on his stogie, trickled smoke out of his nostrils and nodded.

'Yeah, that sounds good.'

'Damned right it's good,' said Mort. 'Now do it.'

Jim finished his drink and with a grunt eased out of his chair. Twenty minutes later, out on the range and seated in his worn saddle, he stared at the far western horizon. Those castellated, rocky tops showed black and gaunt against the star-sprinkled and moonlit sky. Fifteen miles beyond that distant ridge was the town of Rendelo. The majority of its population were still Mexican. Jim also knew that Slash B men whored and drank there on occasion, when things were quiet around the ranch and the ride to Broken Mesa was too much of a chore, for Rendelo was the nearer of the two towns and, on the whole, reached by an easier ride.

In fact, early this evening he had seen Rowdy Mason and Frank Lawson head out for Rendelo and, truth be known, he'd given some thought to joining them. Relaxing in some Rendelo *taberna*, listening to the soft strumming of guitars would make a fine change from the rowdy Broken Mesa drinking houses, and he'd always enjoyed hot Mexican food. He narrowed his eyes. Yup, a trip to Rendelo right now might drag him out of this damned depression he was in.

Then he thought of Dolly Grover and decided there was no contest. At an hour past midnight he entered Broken Mesa and reined down his chestnut gelding to an easy walk and headed up Broad Street.

Dolly Grover's neat, white-painted clapboard house was on the northern edge of town. Reaching it, he eased his horse around the back, dismounted and led it towards Dolly's stable block. There were three stalls in all, as well he knew. Dolly's roan occupied the first stall. The other two compartments were empty.

Dolly's piebold mare had its head out of the open top part of the half-doors. As he passed, it sniffed and whinnied softly when it saw Jim's big chestnut gelding. His ride returned the greeting with what appeared to be happy, snorted enthusiasm.

Jim led his beast to the trough first, then into the next stall. He unsaddled it, groomed it, and fed hay into the iron rack. After that he left for the house, circling around it to reach the front door.

At this time of night no lights shone through Dolly's polished, glazed windows. He rapped on the door then rapped again, louder this time. That brought a reaction. An upstairs lamp was turned up. He watched the light move down the stairs casting all manner of shadows, then he heard the soft padding of slipper-covered feet crossng the hall floor. The main door opened, then the fly door and there stood Dolly, staring out, lamp raised. In her early forties, Dolly was still a handsome woman with a neat figure and auburn hair that, at the moment, hung in a glossy cascade halfway down her back. Her green, inviting eyes lit up the moment she saw him.

'Jim!' she said.

The Slash B *segundo* removed his battered, sweat-stained brown Stetson and grinned. 'Howdy, Dolly; hope it ain't too late for a man to come callin'?'

'Not when it's you,' she said.

Dolly stepped back to allow him to enter, then closed both doors. She led him into the parlour. After she had put the lamp down on to the polished mahogany table she turned, sighed, came into his arms and kissed him hungrily. But after moments, she stepped back and punched him on the arm.

69

'Damn you!' she said. 'It's been too long.'

Jim held his grin. 'But worth the wait, uh?'

She looked at him in that coy way she had. 'Maybe. You hungry?'

He made to take her in his arms. 'For you, yes.' But smiling, Dolly stepped back and pressed her right hand on his chest.

'Easy there, cowboy, a lady usually requires some warning that her white knight intends to come a-callin'.'

'And you got it,' he said with an innocent look. 'I knocked, didn't I?'

'Damn you!'

Then she chuckled and again punched him lightly before turning to the two decanters on the side cupboard. One said whiskey, the other brandy.

'Usual poison?' she said.

'Uh, huh.'

Jim settled into the nearby cushioned settee and crossed his long legs. He watched her pour the whiskey. After a generous quantity had been decanted into each glass she turned and came towards him.

'Then what?' she said as she handed him the passable distillation. He took a swallow, smacked his lips appreciatively and then grinned up at her.

'Well, I'd kind of like to see if you've changed your bed sheets lately.'

She sat down beside him and again punched him, seriously this time. 'Damn you, Jim Alston,' she said, 'is that the kind of thing to say to a lady you ain't seen for more'n a month?'

Though it hurt, he grinned. 'Fits the bill, don't it? Anyway, I'm kind of tired, honey. Ain't been sleeping too well lately'

'The granger business?' she said, serious now.

'I guess.'

A frown creased her brow. 'Yeah, I read it in the *Broken Mesa Courier* – 'bout the trial, that is, and those dreadful things done to the Cadman family. Jim, are they really true? Were you there?'

Jim sighed. 'I was but I tried my damnedest to talk Mort out of it.'

She shook her head and turned away from him, looked into her shot glass.

'You need to get away from that man, Jim,' she said, 'I mean it. If you do I might even consider marrying you.'

'It ain't as easy as that,' Jim said. 'Mort and me . . . well, we go way back, real *amigos*. What happened to his wife and two daughters and the boys unhinged him for a spell; made him so crazy he didn't seem to know right from wrong any more. I tried to pull him out of it but' – Jim sighed – 'well, he seems all right now. Nevertheless, I got to admit that don't hardly mitigate what he did.'

Dolly swung round to face him; her green eyes flashed.

'He's an arrogant, murdering, ruthless bully,' she said, 'always has been, and deep down you know it. And that isn't only my opinion.'

Jim stared at her. 'Easy now, honey, you don't know him like I do. He ain't like that at all . . . usually.'

'Excuses!' Dolly sighed. She leaned over, put her arms around his broad chest and gently laid her head on his breast. 'Oh, Jim, you look all hollowed out. For God's sake leave him; come to me. We'll make out.'

Jim pursed his lips, laid a gentle hand on her right cheek.

'Honey, it ain't that easy,' he said. 'You is fully aware I know nothin' about runnin' a steakhouse. I just know cattle an' horses.'

Dolly's brows made an indignant arch.

'You can learn, dammit!'

Jim toyed with his glass. He had often thought about the offer. It had been put to him before, more than once. Nevertheless, he also knew that Mort would always be an obstacle. At one time he had hoped she would change her mind if she got to know Mort a little better, would marry him and come to live at the ranch. Mort had even offered to have a cabin built for them.

But she did not want to be anywhere near his friend. She did not want to know him, not even a smidgen. Her mind was completely closed to the idea. Mort, to Dolly Grover, was hostile territory.

Jim heaved a sigh. But, dammit, he'd not ridden all this way to talk about Mort Basset, he'd come to lighten up a little, forget about Slash B and his personal troubles for a spell. He had come to relax, for chris'sake!

He looked into Molly's soft green eyes and gently lifted her fine, creamy chin with his calloused index finger.

'You figure that bed of yours is still warm?' he said. 'Looks as though you just left it.'

As he said it, he grinned. It could be a roguish grin, he knew. But this time it did not work. She turned her back on him and said,

'I'm not here just for your convenience, Jim Alston; not any more.'

The end remark was like a punch in the gut, but he quickly recovered. He pulled her gently to him, buried his nose into the back of her sweet-smelling auburn hair. All

72

flippancy left him as the hunger came.

'Please, honey, I need you. You're all I've got. I love you, real hard. You know that.'

She turned abruptly to face him and sighed, as if now helpless to resist him.

'Oh! What am I to do with you, Jim Alston?'

'Take me to bed?' He tried another grin.

She punched him again, fiercely. 'Damn you! Damn you! Damn you!' Then she sighed and capitulated and allowed him to carry her to bed.

CHAPTER ELEVEN

There was a banging on the outer door. Jim rolled over, sleep still thick upon him. 'You answering that, honey?' he said.

Eyes still closed he fumbled around blindly to find her warm body which, he was convinced, should be next to him.

It wasn't.

He sat up, still dazed after a long sleep, and stared around the frill-adorned bedroom. The smell of Dolly Grover's lavender was a heady perfume on the air. Through the drawn, pink, frilly curtains he could see the mid-morning sun was trying to blaze light into the room.

The knocking became insistent, thumps now rather than a normal tapping. He struggled out of bed.

'Goddamnit,' he bawled, 'can't a man get some sleep?'

He saw his clothes were neatly folded on the chair by the dressing table that had a fancy mirror backing it.

Once more, knocking rattled the outer door. Real angry now, Jim awkwardly climbed into his clothes.

'I'm coming!' he roared.

He stamped down the stairs. When he opened the main

door and peered through the mesh of the fly door he saw it was the tall, broad-shouldered and stem-faced county sheriff, Talbot Dixon.

'Heard you came into town late last night,' the lawman said, 'so I figured you'd be here.'

He turned his head and spat brown juice on to Dolly's showy flowerbed.

'Now some people would call that pretty slick detective work, wouldn't you say?' he continued.

Ignoring Dixon's ridiculous self-praise, Jim stared guiltily, out beyond Dolly's white-painted picket fence to the quiet backstreet beyond. But why he should feel sensitive about anyone witnessing his presence here escaped him; Dolly's and his relationship was well known in town. They had never tried to hide it. However, a quick glance told him the area was, to all intents and purposes, deserted.

Now he drew his gaze back to the two ground-hitched horses standing on the other side of Dolly's white fence.

The big roan he recognized as Dixon's. But the chestnut standing, head drooped, alongside it was far more interesting. It had a body lying face down over the saddle. The brand on the chestnut's rump was Slash B.

Jim stared at the determined features of the lawman. A quarter-inch of light-brown stubble sprouted on Dixon's aquiline features, which were deeply grooved on each side and looked as though they had been carved out of buffalo hide. Dixon's eyes were noticeably arresting, too. They were slits the colour of blue ice and appeared to take in every inch of a man, missing nothing. He certainly looked what Jim knew him to be – a tough, no-nonsense lawman. Jim nodded toward the patiently waiting horses the other side of the white paling.

'Well? What gives?'

'Rowdy Mason,' Dixon said. 'Thought you ought to know.'

Jim frowned. 'Dead?'

'Don't he look it?' Dixon said.

'How? Where, dammit?' Jim said, made impatient by the caustic reply.

'Mile outside Rendelo,' Dixon said. 'Couple of passing Messicans found him early this morning, strung up by the neck like a chicken. Lynched I guess you could call it. Those Mexes beat their mule near dead to ride in to tell me.' The lawman paused to fumble in his right shirt pocket. He pulled out a piece of crumpled paper and waved it.

'Another thing,' he added. 'This here note was pinned to my office door when I got back from bringing in Mason's body. Guess you'd better read it. I figure most of the townsfolk already have, but unfortunately nobody saw who pinned it there – or they ain't inclined to say.'

Jim took the piece of paper out of the lawman's hand. The contents were written in block capitals: TELL SLASH B HELL'S A COMIN'.

He frowned at Dixon. 'What's that supposed to mean?'

The lawman pursed lips, lifted sandy brows. 'Revenge, maybe?'

Jim stared. 'For what, dammit?'

The lawman shrugged. He stood hipshot, pulled out the makings and commenced rolling a quirly.

'I've got a theory,' he said. 'Rowdy was one of the lynch party that attended Cadman's death, wasn't he?' When the tube containing the tobacco was formed he licked paper and sealed it before he added,

'Seems a kind of rough justice has been served here, wouldn't you say?' He stuck the makings in his mouth, flipped a match alight with the nail of his thumb and ignited the tobacco. Then he pinched the match out with thumb and finger and dropped it to the ground. He inhaled deeply before he raised brows, as if in enquiry regarding his comments.

Jim glared. 'Rough justice?' he said. 'I thought the law was supposed to run down murderers . . . protect people, not condemn them.'

Dixon once more raised his brows. 'Oh! I'll hunt the culprit down, don't fret,' he said. 'But sometimes, depending on the circumstances, o' course, I'm inclined to do some things with a little less enthusiasm.'

'Damnation! An' you admit to that?' Jim said, his tone loaded with disbelief. 'Well there's one thing for sure. Mort isn't going to be happy about this. In his way, he cares for his men.'

Again Dixon raised sandy brows. 'Is that a fact now?' Not attempting to hide his cynicism he added, 'Real quaint.'

Fired up, Jim stepped down off the stoop. He pushed past Dixon. He went straight to Rowdy's body. He lifted the man's head and stared into his purple, bloated features, then into the wide, staring brown eyes. The livid rope burns around Rowdy's neck were clearly visible. There was also a big gash on the top of his head, from which blood had run freely but was now dry. It looked as though Rowdy had been hit with something heavy before being strung up. Jim gently lowered the head. *Strung up, just like Cadman was.*

Dixon was now standing alongside him. Jim stared at him and said, 'You getting a posse out?'

Dixon spat grey into the dust, then took a drag from his cigarette, inhaled before exhaling and speaking through the blue-grey smoke issuing forth.

'Yup,' he said. 'My chief deputy, George Smith, is on it right now. We figure to be riding out about an hour and a half from now, after the town men forming the posse have had time to pack food, water and make arrangements to cover their business interests during their absence.'

Here Dixon paused and narrowed his eyes. 'I reckon the hunt might take at least a couple of days, maybe more.' The lawman once more stopped and met Jim's gaze. 'You'll be riding along, I guess?'

'I'm the Slash B *segundo*,' Jim said, still fuming, 'of course I'll be along.'

'Are you letting Basset know?'

'He'll know soon enough,' Jim said. 'News, particularly bad news, travels fast in Wild Horse Basin.'

Dixon nodded. 'Yup, got to agree on *that*,' he said. He gave Jim a keen look. 'Well, I'll leave Mason to you. Got things to do. Besides, I'm choosy about the company I keep.'

Hearing that unwarranted insult, Jim formed his calloused hands into fists.

'By God, mister,' he said, 'you're treading a fine line here.'

'Think so?' Dixon's stare was cold. 'Well, I reckon a fellow who can watch a man hanged without cause, watch the fellow's wife and two children burn to death and don't do a thing about it has neither my sympathy nor my regard.'

Jim flared, 'Damn you, I tried to stop it! You know that!'

'Not hard enough, seems to me,' said Dixon. He rolled his half-smoked quirly to the left corner of his mouth, mounted and wheeled his horse. He rode off toward Broken Mesa's main street.

Silently fuming, Jim got his horse out of Dolly's neat, small stable block. He led it out, saddled up, then climbed upon its back and rode it round the front of the house to the gate. There he took up the chestnut's reins. Hot fury still boiled like a cauldron within him as he thought: *That mean-mouthed son of a bitch, Dixon! Well, to hell with him!*

Leading Rowdy's mount he headed for Jacob Farley's place – the workshop of the town's undertaker and carpenter, situated on Fourth Street. He left Rowdy's body there to be prepared for burial and delivery to Slash B, then rode on to Dolly Grover's steakhouse on Broad Street.

Inside, the place was hot and busy. He ordered coffee, steak, chilli beans and fries. When the food and drink were ready Dolly made a point of serving him herself. As she laid the plate and cup down she said,

'I heard about Rowdy. What are you going to do?'

Jim lifted his brows. 'Ride with the posse, I guess.'

'You'll be coming back tonight?'

Jim took her hand and squeezed it gently. 'Doubt it. But see how it goes, huh?'

Dolly's smooth features became serious and her green eyes intense as she met his gaze.

'Come back alive, Jim; I'd find it hard without you.'

He gently pressed her hand again, even smiled a little though he found no reason to smile at this moment.

I ain't planning on dying yet awhile, sweetheart,' he

said. 'Believe it.'

Dolly seemed satisfied with that and bustled off to take another customer's order. Jim began cutting into his twelve-ounce steak.

While he ate he listened to Errol Crabtree in the back. The black man was singing as he fried steaks, sizzled fries and stirred a recipe of his own invention: a spiced, hot-as-hell, bean-and-chilli concoction that Jim was so partial to and was eating right now. Maisie Crabtree, Errol's wife, while washing crocks, was humming along with him. Jim felt forced to brood on why the pair of them were so damned happy while he was so damned full of misery right now.

That aside, Jim decided Dolly had a highly profitable business going here. Admiring her and loving her for her enterprise, he chewed seriously on his beef. Things could be a lot worse for the ex-*segundo* of the Slash B – if it ever came to that – he decided, than having the handsomest lady in town by his side for the rest of his life and a steady income rolling in. It didn't look too hard a job, frying steaks – maybe they could even open a bar? Now, that was something he *could* handle.

He raised his brows. But dream on, dammit, he thought. He was tied to Slash B and always would be.

And it would be his if Mort went first.

CHAPTER TWELVE

Late afternoon, along with the posse, Jim found himself deep into the north-western foothills. He stared bleakly ahead. It was becoming increasingly clear that the hoof-prints they followed were now going to get a whole lot tougher to detect. Before him stretched a large area of bare grey rock, interspersed with clumps of wind-bent pine and aspen, rooted in infrequent soil-filled fissures.

From the start it had been agreed that the hoofmarks suggested it was a draught horse they were following; because of that all accepted that they must be trailing a sodbuster. However, Jim found he was not prepared to fully accept that premise. The tracks were too obvious, he decided, suggesting that somebody who maybe wanted to incriminate the farmers had laid them down.

Mort?

He dismissed the thought from his mind. For one thing he, Jim Alston, would be the first to know if that was the case. Two: even in the unlikely event that Mort *had* kept that fact secret . . . would he lynch his own man?

Not in a coon's age.

Jim stared at the back of Sheriff Dixon, riding maybe a

couple of yards ahead of him. On an impulse he urged his horse forward. Now alongside the lawman he waved a hand.

'What d'you reckon – the big hoofprints? An attempt to trick us?'

Dixon's grey gaze studied him. 'Put the blame on to the farmers, is that what you're getting at?' The lawman pursed his lips. 'It's a possibility, ain't denyin' it.'

'So, what are you goin' to do about it?' Jim said.

'Continue to do my job,' Dixon said. 'Hopefully without interruption from a lynch man and child-killer.'

Anger flared up in Jim. Why was this son of a bitch prodding him so?

'Damn you, Dixon,' he said, 'move on. Whether you like it or not, Mort, me and the boys were found not guilty in a court of law and you need to settle for that, not hide behind a badge to insult people!'

Apparently unaffected by the words, Dixon spat tobacco juice into the dust

'You figure I need to do that?' He offered a mirthless grin. 'Alston, I need to settle for nothing where Slash B is concerned.'

Jim glared. 'You reckon? Well, right now, mister, it's a Slash B rider that's been murdered. And right now that should be claiming your full attention, instead of wallowing around in your own bitterness because the court didn't hold with your opinion.'

Dixon eased his horse to a stop. Jim met his mean stare as it reached across to engage his.

'With regard to the trail we're following,' the lawman then said, 'd'you know if your pal Mort's been usin' this – this talkin' about stirrin' things up by layin' false trails, suggesting it *might* be settlers doin' this?'

'You're way behind on that one, Dixon,' Jim replied. 'I've already thought on it and I'll give you the answer: would he hang his own man? Hell, no!'

Seemingly unimpressed, Dixon spat more tobacco juice to the ground before sliding his chaw into the pouch of his left cheek. Then he eased his mount into motion again and raised his brows.

'You never can tell with some men – particularly the crazy ones,' he said.

Jim tightened his grip on the reins. Spurred by Dixon's cynicism he said,

'By God, mister, Mort ain't here to defend himself but don't sit easy with that. I can do that for him and to hell with that damned badge you're wearin'!'

'Basset being a pard o' yours, of course.' The lawman smiled but the grin lacked mirth. His face settled back into grim lines. 'But we ain't in this to argue, much as it pleases me so to do. Now, who's the nearest farmer to here, d'you know?'

Jim narrowed his eyes, slightly puzzled by the sudden change in direction the conversation had taken. Had Dixon at last recognized that he was going too far and was now easing off on his acid remarks? Jim doubted it. Even so, he calmed his own temper, pointed a calloused finger and said,

'That'll be Neil Crossman, two miles east, by Big Rock Creek. You suspecting him now?'

'I suspect everybody,' Dixon said, 'until it has been proved otherwise.' With that he dug his knees into his horse's flanks and urged his mount into a canter.

Ten minutes later Jim looked up at the craggy, fir-clad

ridge a mile to his left. It was made mellow-looking by the pale yellow sun, which was now about an hour from setting behind that western horizon. On this flat ground the posse of fifteen tired men he was riding with were now loping along the right bank of Big Rock Creek, on toward Crossman's crude but solidly built abode.

Both outbuildings as well as the cabin, Jim already knew, were constructed of mud-caulked pine boles and spaced out on the flat rise of ground to the east, above, and well clear of, the swift-flowing stream.

Neil Crossman, Jim now observed after eye-searching the wheat- and vegetable-filled acres that spread out from the homestead, was about a quarter of a mile away from the cabin. He was leading a powerful-looking ox into a fenced pasture.

Past observations, made from a distance, had brought Jim to accept that Neil Crossman had put a deal of gruelling hard work into this place since he arrived here three years ago. He could not help but admire the man's efforts.

The beast now being in the pasture, Crossman removed the yoke and traces and placed them outside the field gate. He slid the gate poles across and then waited patiently for the posse to arrive. As they rode toward Crossman, Jim turned to Dixon.

'Reckon the use of oxen lets this fellow out,' he said, 'unless he's got a horse stashed away somewhere.'

Dixon spat brown juice, raised brows and said,

'Seems that way. Now it really is lookin' as if it might be a rancher that done for Rowdy Mason and is trying to make us believe it was some farmer that done it.'

Jim glared. 'Damn you, Dixon, you really got it in for us, ain't you?'

Dixon shrugged. 'Got to consider every angle.'

'Well, dammit, that ain't one of 'em!' Jim said.

'An interesting idea, though, you got to admit,' Dixon replied. He urged his horse into giving a little more speed and Jim kicked in heels to keep up.

After riding the 200 yards or so that stood between the posse and the waiting granger they drew rein and eased their mounts down to a walk. Reaching Crossman, Dixon leaned down and pushed out his right hand. The granger paused for a moment before he stepped forward, took it and shook it firmly. Standard custom having been observed, the lawman said,

'I'm Sheriff Talbot Dixon, Mr Crossman. I'd like to ask you a few questions.'

The sodbuster nodded. 'I know who you are.'

Dixon said, 'Well, that's good. Now, you got a horse?'

Crossman made a face and heaved a deep breath before replying.

'Guess I'm not that fortunate. Got a mule, but generally the ox does the work. Use the mule mostly fer pullin' the wagon, an' ridin' if need be.'

Dixon nodded. 'Useful animals are mules, to be sure. By the way, you seen a man riding past on a draught horse within the past few hours?'

Crossman shook his head. 'Been ploughin'; that takes concentration.' He squinted against the low sun's rays. 'Why, has there been trouble?'

'A Slash B rider's been lynched,' Dixon said.

'Well now,' Grossman said, not appearing to be at all concerned, 'don't seem no end to it, do there?'

'To what?' Dixon said.

'This here business 'tween ranchers and settler folk;

85

glad I'm way up here, out of the way a piece. It's poor land but I make the most off it.'

'You sayin' it could be a granger?' Dixon said.

'Ain't sayin' that at all,' answered Crossman, 'but it's got to be somebody. Avengin' the Cadman family, mebbe? But, whatever, it's no concern of mine. I keep to me and mine.'

'It should be everybody's concern, Mr Crossman,' Dixon said. 'Murder is murder.'

Crossman shrugged broad, powerful-looking shoulders expressing indifference. Dixon compressed his lips, raised his brows a little, then said,

'I see.' He waved a hand. 'You mind if we look around?'

Crossman again shrugged. 'Help yourself, I've got nothin' to hide.'

Apart from the barn, in which was a stack of hay but no horses, Crossman had built a sod john a distance from the house, two sod sheds full of various tools near by, and, of course, the caulked, pine-bole-constructed three-roomed cabin which was planned with the capacity to expand. Jim now noticed the four grubby children, ages ranging from two to eight, he guessed, sitting with their backs to the house wall and staring curiously at the gathered posse-men. Presently a hard-faced woman with a flat, grey-eyed stare appeared at the cabin door. She was poorly dressed. She was wiping her hands on a none-too-clean towel and she was clearly pregnant.

Jim eyed her intently. Sometimes, he figured, the women in this unforgiving country were harder than the men: they had to be.

Searching the house the possemen found that most of the furniture was, apart from a fine pedal organ, home-made. But it became clear to Jim early on, and he suspected to Dixon as well, that they were going to draw a blank here. Though Dixon looked disappointed when he returned from prodding around to talk with the granger, who was now standing in front of his homestead, he said,

Well, thank you for your patience, Mr Crossman. We'll be movin' along now.'

The farmer said, 'Would've asked you to 'light and stay awhile, but we ain't got much, as you can see.'

'We have victuals, Mr Crossman,' Dixon said, 'and we still got an hour's daylight to use. However, I appreciate that the offer is kindly given and, on behalf of my men, I thank you for that.'

'Just thought I'd make it known folks are usually welcome here,' said Crossman.

Dixon produced an amiable smile. 'That is plain, sir,' he said. He touched the brim of his black, worn, low-crowned hat. 'Well, a good day to you and yours.'

He turned to the posse. 'Mount up, boys; time to leave. Maybe we'll make the Crossed N by nightfall.'

Though the Crossed N promised rest and comfortable cover for the night, as Jim well knew, there were groans from the saddle-sore town men. Even so, they gritted their teeth, mounted and fell in behind Dixon as he put his tired horse into a canter. Crossman watched them leave. He spat phlegm.

He made it a wholly disdainful gesture.

CHAPTER THIRTEEN

The posse was now up on the ridge, spread out and moving north, looking for the sign they had lost. Ranging his gaze around him, Jim silently cursed this rough, craggy country. Even more, he cursed the son of a bitch they were trailing, for leading them into such an unforgiving area. The fellow sure knew how to make a trail as difficult as possible to follow, that was for sure. And, Jim guessed also for sure, the fellow had done this several times before.

Three miles on the Crossed N outfit came into view. Jim stared down the mile-long grassy slope that stretched between him and the modest group of ranch buildings he was now scrutinizing. Not unexpectedly, being near to that outfit, a cowpuncher he knew to be Henry Johnson came riding out of a nearby sprawl of rocks fifty yards below him.

Henry spurred, up toward him. Jim waited until Johnson – a week's growth of beard on his lantern jaw and with ragged tufts of brown hair sticking out from under his brown, battered hat – drew rein beside him. Henry was clearly surprised to see him, though he grinned a welcome.

'Howdy, Jim?' he said. 'You're far from home.' Then he nodded toward the other possemen still searching the rock-strewn hillside. 'And seein' them, I take it you got trouble.'

'Found Rowdy Mason hanged this mornin',' Jim said.

Johnson's eyes rounded with amazement under their puffy lid.

'The hell you say! Rowdy . . . *hung*? Who coulda done such a thing?'

'That's what we aim to find out, Henry,' Jim said.

He noticed as they talked that the possemen were dribbling down towards them. When they were gathered around, Dixon, who was last to arrive, spoke, gazing at the Crossed N rider.

'Henry Johnson, isn't it?' he queried.

Henry grinned. 'As ever is.'

Dixon nodded, offered a half-smile. 'You seen a rider on a draught horse passin' by recently, Henry?'

Johnson raised brows. 'Why, yeah; 'bout two hours back.' He turned, pointed to the craggy tops the posse had just come down from. 'I was up there on that ridge lookin' for a cougar that's been givin' us trouble. The fella was pickin' his way through those big rocks down the other side. Naturally, I took him for a sodbuster . . . ridin' thet kinda hoss.'

'Did you recognize him?' Dixon asked.

Henry shook his head. 'Naw. Too far away, I guess: mile, maybe more. Don't know many grangers anyway. But he was pressin' that horse mighty hard.' Henry paused, squinted his eyes. 'He the man you're lookin' for?'

'Could be,' Dixon replied.

'On'y could be, uh?' Henry said.

'So far.'

While the two talked Jim stared up at the black sky to the south. Though the sun was still a glorious, heart-warming orange ball above the western mountain summits amid thin clouds that were streaked with vivid reds, golds and yellows, those thunderheads southward looked menacing. Moreover, their dark bulks were heading straight for Crossed N range. Furthermore, brilliant forked lances of lightning were spearing through those dark immensities, followed, seconds later, by the earth shaking and rumbling booms of thunder. Jim looked at Dixon and nodded.

'That son of a bitch'll be on us within the hour is my guess. Reckon we won't be able to do much about followin' sign in that, dark closin' in an' all.'

Dixon rubbed his bristled chin. 'Inclined to agree.'

Henry Johnson said, brightly, 'Say, why not make yourself at home in one of the ranch barns for the night? Reckon the boss'll make you real welcome. We just don't git many visitors out here.'

Henry's boss, Jim knew, was Hiram Nelson, a man small in stature but solid in bone and muscle, and rawhide tough. Like most ranchers in the basin, he was known to be friendly and hospitable. Though the jury was out on that one when it came to the farmers, Jim decided.

'Invitin',' Dixon said.

But almost drowning out his reply came the pounding of hoofs. All heads swung and eyes stared in the direction the sound was coming from. Less than ten seconds later Mort rounded the nearby stand of pines at the head of a large group of Slash B riders. On reaching the posse, the group pulled rein amid a cloud of dust. Their horses were white with sweat-lather and had clearly been hard used. Unsurprised, Jim looked at his long-time friend and said, with a hint of friendly cynicism,

'What took you so long?'

As usual, Mort went straight to it. 'Cut the humour; what you got?'

Jim shook his head. 'Nothin' yet.'

Mort glared. 'Nothin'?' He half-closed his fat-puffed eyelids and demanded, 'Where you headin' right now?'

'Crossed N,' Jim said. 'Seems no point in goin' on with night closin' in an' that big storm headin' this way.' He pointed at the menacing clouds.

The red in Mort's cheeks heightened to become bright crimson and something akin to thunderheads formed on his brow.

'Well, to hell with that!' he said. 'Jim, we got a Slash B man dead, lynched! Don't that mean anythin' to you?'

Jim glared his resentment. 'Dammit, quit it, you know it does.'

But apparently not noticing Jim's sudden anger, Mort turned in the saddle and yelled, 'Buffalo Killer?'

Jim knew Buffalo Killer to be a Cheyenne scout and general hanger-on around Fort Larson, ten miles south of the basin. Mostly, he scouted for the army when needed but right now it seemed he was riding for Slash B. *Fortuitously passing by Slash B and Mort had asked him to help?* Maybe. Buffalo Killer was noted for riding in on ranches looking for a free meal and maybe a little work but Buffalo Killer usually did not press that side.

The tall Indian came up close. He was a handsome fellow, like most Cheyennes. On his head was a tall black Stetson with an eagle feather stuck in the headband. The rest of his garb was a mix of Indian buckskin and white man's gear. A Bowie knife in a beaded sheath hung from his also beaded belt. He nursed a Winchester rifle to his chest as if it was his most precious possession. Probably it was.

Buffalo Killer said, 'You want me, Bas-set?'

'You reckon you can follow sign in that?' Mort nodded, waved a sweeping gesture at the thunderous sky to the south and the sun, now setting as an orange half-ball below the jagged peaks of the western horizon.

The Cheyenne's dark, narrow features expressed doubt. 'Dark soon,' he said, 'plenty rain coming. Not good.'

'That's not what I asked,' Mort said.

Buffalo Killer shrugged. 'Try, I guess. But horses tired. Lost sign anyhow. Don't make sense. Wait 'til morning, Bas-set. That makes sense.'

Mort glared at the Indian. 'You making damned excuses here?'

The Cheyenne's hawkish brown face stiffened. 'Buffalo Killer don't make excuses,' he said. 'Make sense.'

Dixon said, 'He's right, Basset. It's a crazy idea.'

Mort turned in the saddle, his lips forming a sneer.

'Well now, our famous lawman,' he said. 'Like I allus figured, when it came down to it, not up to the job. Well, we'll see about gettin' you out come next election; that's for sure.'

Dixon's stare glinted like chips of ice. 'Don't throw threats at me, Basset, they don't pay.'

Mort smirked. 'Oh! It ain't a threat, Dixon, believe me; it's a promise.' He turned. Jim met his gaze. 'You riding with us, *compadre*?'

Jim pursed his lips, sucked in breath. 'You know I want to, Mort,' he said, 'but I tend to take Dixon's view.' He nodded at the black-as-hell southern sky. 'That's one big storm brewin' yonder and comin' in fast. I think it would be crazy to try anythin' in that. Our horses are played out, anyway. They need rest. Looks like your riders ain't too healthy, either.'

'Dammit, Jim,' Mort said, 'we got a man dead an'—'

The boom of a big rifle cut off the rest of Mort's words. Casey Lomas, a Slash B rider, who, Jim knew, had also, like Rowdy Mason, been a member of the Cadman hanging party, emitted a harsh cry and crumpled out of the saddle. He hit the ground hard, jerked a few times and then lay still.

Jim immediately turned his startled gaze to the basin's west ridge. Although night had near closed in now, up there, on that rocky pine-clad top, there was still light.

He saw a plume of blue-grey powder smoke drifting north on a light breeze.

He made a quick calculation and figured that the shot had been fired over all of 400 yards. Jim set his chin into a grim line, his reckoning incredulous but undeniable. Whoever pulled that trigger and could lay a trail so hard to follow and could shoot so accurately in this gloom had to be a force to be reckoned with.

Mort's bawling snapped him out of his thoughts. His *amigo* was waving a fierce hand at the startled possemen.

'Hell and damnation, what you waitin' for? Get after that murderin' son of a bitch!'

There was a brief pause before both the possemen and the Slash B seemed to jerk out of their shock, merge and fan out and head for the ridge. However, another booming report echoed across the now panic-loaded evening air. Appalled, Jim stared as Mort's tall grey Stetson flew off his shaggy head. He saw bright blood running now down the side of his friend's shocked, brick-red face. Then, as loose as a sack of potatoes, and with a harsh cry, Mort toppled off his big roan horse and hit the ground hard, there to lie still, while Jim watched in horror.

The riders reined up and looked back, their pallor strikingly white in this fading light. Their startled eyes, looking at Jim, were full of questions: should they stay with Mort, a prominent citizen and the boss of Splash B, or should they pursue his attacker. Clearly they were seeking guidance. Jim gave it.

'Get after that no-good son of a bitch, goddamnit!' he bawled. ' 'Smatter with you?'

Then, carrying his rifle, he swung down off his horse and ran towards Mort. However, as he ran, once more the ominous crack of that rifle up there reverberated across the basin. Another man fell. This time it was Pete Sloan.

A cold hand gripped Jim's stomach. Pete Sloan was another member of the party that had been in on the hanging of John Cadman. It was now becoming clear – that as Dixon had implied this morning, the attacks were definitely selective. Indeed, it was obvious that that bastard up there was out to kill every man jack who had been involved in those South Range killings. Couldn't be any other way.

Now one of the posse was yelling, 'Well, to hell with this, boys, I'm for cover!' Clearly thinking that that was a good idea, the rest of the riders dismounted and scattered to find concealment, carrying their long guns with them.

Jim was about to roar at them when he heard lead hiss

like an angry sidewinder past his head, maybe less that an inch or so away, and again accompanied by the boom of that big rifle up there.

As he went to ground, his heart thumping like a sledge-hammer against his ribs, he came to the opinion that the gun up there was a Sharps 'Big Fifty', a rifle known to have made a killing shot of up to 1,000 yards.

Pressed flat to the ground, cold sweat now dripping off his forehead and down his grim face, Jim ranged his gaze across the rimrock. Again he saw powder smoke drifting on the rising wind. But, giving him some comfort, the long guns of all the riders were roaring their death song and little clouds of rock dust were springing off the grey boulders up there.

Feeling the urgent need to join in, and to hell with dis-obedience, Jim levelled up his rifle, but movement to his left distracted him. Despite the growing gloom, he could just make out the form of Talbot Dixon, riding alone and beating his horse to try and drag out every last ounce of running left in it, to force it to dash up the long slope to the rimrock and cover.

What was the crazy fool doing?

Jim began to deliver murderous fire aiming his Winchester towards where he'd last seen the ambusher's gunsmoke. He continued to pour out lead, giving the lawman cover until he achieved the top of the ridge and disappeared over it. Then Jim sank down, pressed his body against the sweet-smelling grass. His hot rifle now being empty, he began to reload. As he did so, he saw a rider erupt half a mile down the top of the ridge and gallop away north. It had to be the ambusher. But riding a fresh saddle horse?

And got from where?

Jim's hopes of the possibility of kill or capture died. There was no way Dixon, even though the lawman was now up there, or anybody else for that matter, would be able to catch that murderous son of a bitch. All the posse and Slash B horses were played out. But it was a desperately crushing admission to make now that they'd got this close.

Full of anger because of that, and feeling disgusted at the helplessness he felt, he turned his attention to Mort.

His friend of many years was still out cold and blood was leaking from what looked to be a deep bullet crease that ran along the right side of his head. It did not appear to be life threatening, but Mort was going to have one hell of a headache when he woke up, that was for sure.

Right there, his attentions were interrupted by more thunderclaps, much closer. This time the earth shook. Lightning was cutting dazzling patterns across the sky, overhead this time, and was increasing in frequency. On top of that, the wind was building up, causing the trees to thresh about wildly. Jim now had no doubts that this was going to be one humdinger of a storm and the sooner they got themselves and the horse into shelter the better.

But Dixon was still up on that ridge. . . .

He should go after him. There was always a chance that son of a bitch had somehow lost his mount and. . . .

He closed down on his thoughts. No way. Crazy thinking. First, he must check on the men who had been shot.

He quickly established that Casey Lomas was dead, due to a half-inch hole that had been drilled through the middle of his forehead, in consequence of which the back of his head had been blasted out in a mess of blood and brains. There was nothing that could be done for the man, apart from bury him decent. On the other hand Pete Sloany, though hit in the chest and bleeding badly, was still alive. By his side was Cory Thomas, a Slash B rider, busy trying to stem the flow of blood with his bandanna. Jim pressed Cory's shoulder and said, 'Do what you can for him, huh, Cory.'

Thomas stared up. 'Goes without saying, Jim.'

The Slash B *segundo* nodded. 'Yeah, guess it does.'

He was making his way back to Mort when there was another distant boom of a rifle. It came from the back of the ridge this time. He instinctively ducked. But nobody dropped dead and no lead hissed by. Was it Dixon taking a shot at the ambusher, or was the rifleman attempting to put an end to all pursuit by downing Dixon? It had to be one or the other.

Jim turned to Frank Lawson, who was crouching close by and staring hard at the ridge's now almost dark summit. Having got the cowpuncher's attention Jim said,

'Frank, get help and get Mort and the rest of the dead and the wounded – as well as the rest of the men – down to the Crossed N. I'm going after Dixon.'

Lawson frowned and stared his doubt.

'The hell you are? Dammit, take it easy up there, Jim. Four Slash B men down in one day's enough. Let Dixon take care of himself.'

'Inclined to agree,' said Jim, 'but it's what I have to do. I heard shots up there.'

CHAPTER
FOURTEEN

He mounted and made a wide loop to the left to gain the top of the ridge, then dropped down into the cover of the rocks and pines on the other side.

Once there Jim paused, listened and peered into the gloom ahead. By now, twilight was almost gone and the wind was growing more powerful by the minute. It roared and hissed, tossing the pines about as if they were mere stems of grass. Streaks of lightning were now directly above and drilling brilliant lances of white light across the black sky before earthing. Thunder rolled and boomed, almost continuously now. Near by, startling Jim, a tree split with a loud crack as lightning ripped it apart to leave a smouldering jagged gash, which was immediately extinguished by the rain that was now lashing down.

His face now was streaming with rainwater, his hat and clothes were soaked, but Jim urged his mount on, all the time staring ahead. His rifle was clasped in his big, bony right hand, ready to be brought into instant action should the need arise, but there was nary a sign of either man or beast. But he kept looking.

Startling him, Dixon came walking out of the gloom and driving rain. His saddle was draped over his left shoulder, his old Henry rifle clasped in his right hand. Quick as a mountain cat Dixon dropped his saddle, lifted his rifle and lined it up. Alarm coursed through Jim. He lifted his arms.

'Easy, goddamnit,' he called, 'it's me . . . Alston!'

The sheriff hesitated a moment, then he lowered his long gun and peered through the torrent of rain.

'The hell you doin' here?' he said.

'Nice to see you, too,' Jim said. Then he grinned, finding a certain delight in Dixon's predicament. 'Afoot, huh?'

Dixon glowered up at him. 'Son of a bitch shot my horse out from under me. Seems you're pleased about that.'

Jim raised dark brows. 'Not particularly,' he said. 'Real question is, why didn't he kill *you*? He's been trying his best to send the rest of us to salvation.'

Dixon passed a long-fingered left hand over his wet, bristled face and glowered through the dark.

'Because, like I said this morning, he don't want me,' he said, 'he wants the bunch that lynched Cadman and burnt his family.'

Anger burnt into Jim. 'There you go agin! Are you celebrating that?'

Dixon shook head, a serious look on his dripping face.

'No,' he said, 'I'm a lawman and I'll do my job. And – mebbe surprising you – on the whole I'm agin killin'. It makes the job more difficult. Nevertheless, you recall what was written on the note that was pinned to my office door this mornin'?'

'Tell Slash B hell's a comin'?' Jim said. 'What about it?'

Dixon pursed his lips. 'Well, right now,' he said, 'I'd say Satan's horde's arrived with a vengeance, wouldn't you?'

Jim stared at the dripping lawman. He was standing, his saddle now back on his left shoulder, his rifle in his right hand, while sheets of rain splashed on and around him. That was a damned brutal thing for Dixon to say, Jim decided. However, he was already suspecting, though he was loath to admit it, that Dixon was right. Three men hit, one dead and another probably by now, and Mort bleeding from a bullet crease; it had to be about the Cadman business. Damn Mort Basset. Reluctantly, he made a stirrup free to step into and said,

'Well, you'd better climb up, Dixon, I'm gittin' soaked sittin' here.'

Dixon stared for a moment, as if surprised, then swung up his sodden saddle. 'Here, catch a holt of this, will you?'

Jim held the proffered saddle while the sheriff climbed up behind him. As Dixon took back the worn saddle he said,

'You're a strange mix, Alston. Why did you come lookin' for me?'

'Don't read anything into it,' Jim said, 'I'd do the same for a dog.'

For some reason Dixon laughed, heartily. But not wanting to analyse the reaction, or ask why, Jim grouchily urged his tired horse through the dark and the lightning and the thunder and the seemingly interminable lashing rain, which had already drenched them through and through. He headed down the slippery slope and on towards the warm yellow light showing through the windows of the Crossed N.

When they rode into the ranch's confines they found that the men had made themselves comfortable in the two barns which Hiram Nelson had made available. Brannan Crenshaw, normally a cleaner at the Thirsty Man saloon but who had once been a trail cook, preparing slop for the men driving beeves up the Chisholm Trail, was getting food ready, using the ranch cookhouse to do it. It was plain trail fare, gleaned from what feed was in the posse men's saddle-bags, but palatable enough.

Already Dixon and Jim had learnt that Esther Nelson, Hiram Nelson's comely, shiny-cheeked wife, had tended to Mort's head wound. Pete Sloan did not need attention, it was said, apart from burying, that was. He'd died on the way down to the ranch. Mort, they were informed, was now, after Esther's earnest ministrations, stretched out in one of the children's bedrooms, fast asleep with four large slugs of Hiram's personally brewed distillation in his gut. Jim shook his head. Two more dead; how many more would there be, and would he be among them?

With his horse curried and fed, Jim was now standing with Talbot Dixon in the larger of the two Crossed N barns with a plateful of the tasty food that Brannan Crenshaw had conjured up. He saw Hiram Nelson talking animatedly to a couple of Slash B riders. Presumably Nelson wanted to know the latest news concerning Broken Mesa, as well as the cause of all the shooting trouble up on the ridge.

When Hiram saw them he grinned and came over, but before he could speak, Jim said,

101

'Will Mort be fit to ride tomorrow?'

Nelson shrugged, pursed his lips and furrowed his brow.

I'm not a doctor, but he's a tough customer, Jim, as well you know.'

Despite the non-committal answer Jim felt a sense of relief.

'That's for sure.' He raised his brows. 'Well,' he indicated the plate of food in his hand, 'when I've eaten this I reckon I'll get some shut-eye.'

'Kind of like that idea, too,' said Dixon. 'Been a long day.'

Five minutes later, nestled in the sweet-smelling hay and divested of most of his sopping wet clothes, Jim prepared for sleep. The storm roared furiously out there, the rain beat against the barn walls with a constant tattoo. It did not affect him. He soon sank into an exhausted sleep. Dixon was already snoring near by.

CHAPTER FIFTEEN

Seven hours later Jim woke to see through the open barn door that the sun's already hot rays were beating down and steam was rising from the puddled, soggy ground. With Dixon he dressed quickly and stepped out. He quickly found that the steam's clamminess was unpleasant and stuck to his face as if it was dank paper.

He did his best to ignore the vapours and went across to the cookhouse, where he helped himself to a breakfast of flapjacks, syrup, and fatty bacon placed between two slices of Esther Nelson's wholesome dark-brown bread. Still with Dixon, he then gathered his horse and saddled it.

Then he left Dixon to organize the posse while he went to look for Mort. He found his *amigo* in front of the house, trying his damnedest to mount his horse. He was obviously too ill to do it: he staggered back and fell to the ground.

'Take the day off, dammit,' Jim said, riding up.

Mort stared up at him. His face was pale and drawn and tired-looking.

'Ain't good at takin' advice, as you know, old friend,' he said, 'but this time' – he sighed and shook his head – 'well,

I guess I'm gonna have to.'

That was new, Jim thought, and the admission worried him a little. However, he said,

'Damned right you do.'

Hiram Nelson now came out of the house and ran down the stoop steps.

'Told him not to try it,' he said angrily, 'but he wouldn't listen.'

'You surprised by that, Hiram?' Jim asked.

'No!' Nelson replied. Then he gently assisted Mort up the steps and across the stoop to the open door, where Esther stood waiting. She took over and helped Mort into the house.

'Guess he'll make his mind up what he'll do when he feels able,' Jim said.

Hiram nodded. 'Knowin' Mort Basset to be an ornery cuss, that's how it'll be, I guess,' he said. Jim smiled and touched the brim of his worn Stetson.

'Well, *adios* for now, Hiram, and thank you for your hospitality.'

The rancher waved a dismissive hand. 'Welcomed the company. Now, you just see you catch that murdering son of a bitch, y'hear?'

'We'll get him,' Jim replied through lips set into a grim line.

Along with the two posses Dixon had now rounded up, he turned his horse and headed for the ridge two miles up the long aspen-and-pine-strewn slope that reared up from the flat valley bottom.

Buffalo Killer had already departed at early dawn to look for sign. He joined them half an hour later as they made their way across the rocky ground at the back of the ridge. Right off, the stone-faced Indian picked out Dixon.

'No sign of saddle horse,' he said, 'rain wash away. But sign of big horse . . . left deeper tracks.' He narrowed his eyes. 'We follow, uh?'

Dixon's lean face tightened up. He nodded, grimly. 'We do,' he said. 'Got to lead somewhere.'

But Jim soon discovered it was a painstaking business riding this rocky terrain. The slow progress they made trying to pick up further sign was getting to be more than a tad frustrating. On top of that, the clammy heat that still persisted had become a real nuisance. Nevertheless, the sweating posse appeared to accept the discomfort, but by no means graciously. An hour later they again lost sign and Buffalo Killer was sent out once more, looking for tracks. A clearly frustrated Dixon pulled rein.

'Well,' he said, 'we might as well eat and rest the horses for a while.'

An hour later they were preparing to ride again when Buffalo Killer rejoined them. He was chewing blackberry-sweetened pemmican and was taking occasional sips of water. Once more the Indian made straight for Dixon.

'Found good sign now,' he said. 'Not lose again.'

'We'll see,' said Dixon. He turned to what was now one posse of twenty-five men. 'Right, boys, let's get to it.'

Two hours later they looked down on what Jim knew to be the Freeman homestead. It was a neat place with a variety of crops growing in the well-tilled fields. But even more interesting, Jim thought, was the sight of a big draught horse in the corral at the side of the small barn. When Dixon saw it he perked up.

'Well now,' he said. He raised sandy brows and Jim met his eager look. 'Luke Freeman claimed to be Cadman's friend, remember? Took the bodies fer buryin', you recall?' Dixon pointed to a distant rise of ground. 'He buried the whole family atop of that hill. I know because I attended the burial.'

'You saying Freeman could be the killer?' Jim asked.

'Rule nothin' out; that's my motto,' Dixon answered.

Jim noticed three children as they rode in. One, a boy, was weeding the large fenced vegetable patch at the back of the cabin, while the two smaller ones, girls, were sweeping off the stoop with besoms. Luke Freeman, Jim saw, was sawing logs, which, he assumed, were destined to become winter fuel. The granger stopped sawing when he saw the posse approaching and, frowning, mopped his brow while waiting for them to arrive.

When the posse got close and pulled rein amid a large group of clucking hens pecking at the bare soil in front of the cabin, without ado Dixon nodded toward the draught horse in the corral, which was pulling at the nearby full hay bag hanging from a pole.

'That horse yours?' he asked.

Freeman nodded. 'Yup,' he replied, 'somebody took it. It came back of its own accord this morning, praise be to the Lord. Mighty glad to have him back. I surely would be lost without him. Lots of heavy work to be done.'

'Who took him?' said Dixon.

'That I do not know.'

'You reported him stolen?'

Freeman shook his head. 'No,' he said. 'It's a long way to town. I'd got no horse and three children. Been waiting for someone to pass by, but no need now.'

Dixon grunted, shifted himself in his saddie. Sweat patches were very much in evidence on the back of his green-and-cream-striped shirt and under his arms; the rest of the posse were in similar case.

'Well, I'll get straight to the point, Freeman,' the lawman said. 'That horse has been involved in a killin'.'

Freeman frowned. 'How do you know that, and what has a killing got to do with me, pray?'

'I take it you're not a complete fool,' Dixon said testily, 'and you claim it's your horse. Well, we've been following the animal all the way from the scene of the crime, so figure the answer out for yourself.'

Freeman nodded. 'The horse is indeed mine,' he said. 'However, if you think I killed somebody you are badly mistaken. The Bible clearly says: "thou shalt not kill" and I follow that commandment to the letter.' He paused, raised dark brows. 'I am a man of God, Sheriff Dixon, and I follow the Bible's teachings.'

He paused once more and turned to the children who were standing near by, curiosity clearly expressed on their dirty faces while they shyly watched and listened intently to the proceedings.

Freeman gestured. 'And I have three children to look after. Would I jeopardize them by doing such a foolish thing?'

'You've got a wife,' said Dixon. 'You claimed to have been a friend of Cadman's. You've got reason to kill.'

'My wife is away,' Freemen said.

Dixon stared. '*Away?*'

'Yes.' Freeman's look turned bitter, then he went on, 'Jane Cadman and the two children who were burned along with her . . . they were my wife's sister, my sister-in-law and the two girls were obviously, our nieces.' The granger paused. He now seemed to be having trouble in keeping control of his emotions. After moments, as if to brace himself, he lifted his square, bristled chin and went on.

'As you can imagine my wife is greatly grieving the loss, as am I; but the hurt is much greater for her. So much so that she has gone to be with her kinfolk in Cheyenne. I expect she will be gone for some time.'

'*Cheyenne?*' said Dixon. 'That's a mean place.'

'The Lord will take care of her,' Freeman said, calmly and confidently.

Here Jim decided he should take part, and he stared down at the granger from atop his horse.

'And you let her go with a big place like this to run,' he queried, 'and with three children to look after?' He leaned forward. 'Am I hearing aright here? Isn't there mail she could've used?'

Freeman said, 'The Lord guided us in our decision.'

'The hell he did,' Jim said. 'The Lord be damned!'

Freeman stared, clearly shocked and angry.

'I will ask you not use blasphemy here, sir,' he said. 'It is what happened.' Then he paused and pointed at Jim with a calloused right index finger. 'And you, sir, and the persons you associate with, were responsible for that decision.'

The granger now jutted his lean, square chin even more firmly and squared his shoulders. Jim now saw a suggestion of fanaticism enter Freeman's stern grey gaze as he added,

'But the Lord will punish, never fear; if not in this life, then most certainly He will in the next.'

Anger ripped through Jim. 'I tried to stop it, damn you!'

'Only the Lord will be the judge of that,' Freeman said, calm again.

'Did you send the note?' Dixon asked.

'Note?' Freeman frowned. 'I know of no note.'

'Did you hang Rowdy Mason?' Jim asked.

Freeman stared, looking shocked

'I have hanged nobody.'

'You are personally involved,' Dixon said. 'Kin of Cadman through marriage. You wouldn't be human if you didn't want revenge.'

' "Vengeance is mine," saith the Lord,' Freeman said, 'and I will leave that judgment to Him.'

'Damn your Lord!' Jim burst out. However, he immediately regretted his words. He had been brought up a Christian man and to fear the Lord's wrath should he attempt to use profanity in his name. It was clear this man was still suffering his loss. Jim was now of the opinion that this man was telling the truth. Freeman was staring at him intently, then he said,

'I believe you are a good man at heart, Jim Alston, but, sadly, misguided.'

'Well, this is goin' nowhere,' Dixon said impatiently. He stared at the homesteader. 'I should take you in, but who is to look after the children?'

'There is nobody,' Freeman said, 'and you have no reason to "take me in" as you say. I know nothing of any killings.'

'Three men dead,' Dixon said. 'Mort Basset wounded, all belonging to Slash B. Don't that tell you somethin', Freeman?'

The granger seemed unmoved. 'Still you have no proof. And, as I have already explained, the horse that was stolen returned of its own accord. What it did while it was gone I have no knowledge of and, in any case, would I leave my children here, alone, to go hunting for killers? Who is being the fool here?'

'Don't try insulting me, Freeman,' said Dixon, a hard edge to his tone, 'that wouldn't be wise. Now, I need to search your house.'

Freemen shrugged and waved a hand. 'Be my guest. I have nothing to hide.' And he didn't. The house, barn, john, shed were clean of any evidence to suggest Freeman was the killer of Rowdy Mason, Pete Sloan, Casey Jones and the wounding of Mort Basset. They found a Winchester rifle in the house, but no Spencer .50, the rifle Jim was sure was used to kill two men and wound Mort. However, he felt he needed to say something.

'What's with the rifle, if you're a man of peace?'

'The Lord is ever bountiful,' Freemen said. 'He provides game for the sustenance of men and their families.'

Jim scowled but could not disagree. Dixon sighed and dropped his shoulders.

'Well,' he said, 'we're wasting our time here. We need to retrace.'

Buffalo Killer spoke, a little despondently. 'No find sign first time; not likely to find second time,' he suggested.

Dixon glared at him. 'We still look, damn it!'

The Cheyenne shrugged. 'Buffalo Killer take white man's dollar all day,' he said. 'No skin off his hide.' He grinned, broadly.

It took another grueling two days searching under a searing sun before Dixon called off the hunt. And an hour after midnight on the fifth day, dirty and bedraggled, the mixed posse entered Broken Mesa. The townsfolk peeled away to their homes as they rode down Main Street. But the Slash B contingent, when they reached the still open Mighty Fine saloon, entered the drinking place amid tired mumbles of approval and slaked their thirst with quantities of pale warm beer. Not much talk passed between them and the few people still in the saloon – mostly card players – did not bother them with questions for it was obvious the cowmen were bone tired and looking mighty disinclined to answer questions.

After Jim had downed his third schooner he said, 'Well, let's make for home, boys.' Alfred Jones, long-time rider for the Slash B, said with heart-felt fervour, 'Well, amen to that. I could sleep for a week.'

Long murmurs of concurrence followed the comment.

CHAPTER SIXTEEN

Neither Jim nor the crew were ready for what they found a mile along the trail that led to Slash B. Mace Brandon was hanging by the neck from the bough of a cottonwood.

Closer inspection suggested that Mace's head, like Rowdy Mason's, had been caved in from behind with something heavy before he was hauled up.

A bunch of nerves nibbled at Jim's gut. Straight away it struck him that Mace Brandon was yet another of those who had been involved in the hanging of John Cadman and the burning of his cabin, along with the terrible incineration of Cadman's wife and two children. Once more he recalled the message that had been pinned to Sheriff Dixon's office door:

TELL SLASH B HELL'S A COMIN'.

Jim compressed his thin lips. As Dixon had already pointed out – and he now went along with it – somebody was out for revenge and this latest killing seemed to confirm that assumption. Jim's grey eyes took on a new, hard edge as he drew his Bowie knife and cut through the hang rope.

An hour later, in front of the Slash B ranch house, he

dismounted. Lights were already coming on in the large building. Moments later he saw Mort appear at the door and stride out on to the long veranda that fronted the dwelling. Jim saw that Mort's head was still heavily bandaged, but the Slash B boss carried his Winchester and was clearly ready to use it, if needs be.

Mort lowered the rifle when he saw the posse, which was already dispersing to strip off saddles and wipe down horses before corralling them and giving them water and hay.

Mort stared down at him.

'Well?' he said eagerly, 'did you catch him?'

Jim shook his head. 'Seen neither hide nor hair. Must have got himself a real fast mount when he ditched the draught horse.'

Mort scowled. 'Damn.' Then he peered into the night gloom. 'Who's that you got over the saddle?'

'Mace Brandon; found him hanging trailside.'

Mort's body stiffened. For the first time in years Jim saw worry lines crease themselves across Mort's brow.

'Dammit,' he said, 'who is this son of a bitch, Jim?'

'Whoever he is he's making a damn fool of us. Brandon makes four dead now; all of them men who were in on the Cadman business – and I'm not including your near miss. How *is* your head, by the way?'

'Aches like a bitch and getting worse,' Mort said. Then he frowned. 'You saying these are revenge killings?'

Jim stared his amazement. 'Well, ain't they?' he said. 'That's what Talbot Dixon thinks, too.'

Mort scowled his fierce dislike of the law at the mention of his name. Jim knew that Mort had not forgotten or forgiven Dixon's strident courtroom opposition to Slash B's getting cleared of the Cadman business, and his opinion had been that the death sentence should be served on the Slash B owner and at least fifteen years apiece for the crew for standing by and allowing the killings to happen.

'He does, huh?' Mort said. 'Does he know about Mace Brandon?'

'No,' Jim replied. 'I didn't go back to town. The men are bone tired and anyway, what's the point? The speed news travels in the basin Dixon'll know all about this come tomorrow, mebbe sooner.'

'Yeah, I guess,' Mort agreed. He hauled himself up to his full, powerfully built five feet ten. 'Jim, we've got to nail this bastard before he kills any more Slash B crew. First thing in the morning we go look for sign, and this time hope it leads to something.'

'We'll have to let Dixon know,' Jim said.

Mort raised his brows. 'Him bein' the law, huh?' He sighed and dolefully shook his head. 'Goddamn, what's happened to the old days, Jim?'

'Dead, and you know it,' Jim told him.

Mort scowled. 'Well, I don't like it,' he said. 'Range justice still fills the bill for me.' He leaned forwards. 'Your search found nothing, uh?' he said as if he needed to have the bad news fully confirmed. He shook his head. 'This is some greasy son of a bitch we're chasin', Jim, for sure.'

Jim nodded his agreement. 'The draught-horse tracks led to that granger Freeman's place. He said the horse had been stolen and it had returned of its own accord.' Jim now met Mort's sharp stare and added, 'He's on his own out there, Mort, with three young children to look after. He said his wife is the sister of Cadman's wife and that she has been made real grief-stricken by the deaths of her sister and their two nieces, as he has also been. She has gone back home to Cheyenne to grieve with her family.'

Mort glared. 'And that son of a bitch is blamin' us for what happened? Dammit, Cadman shootin' that beeve and cuttin' off that haunch brought that grief on that man's family, not us.'

Jim shrugged. 'Mebbe. Anyway, he says he's had nothing to do with the killin's goin' on; claims he is a man of God and that vengeance belongs to the Lord, not him.'

'Pah!' Mort growled.

Jim shrugged again. 'He was also keen to point out that, in any case, he would not leave his children alone to go seek retribution.' Jim looked directly at Basset. 'I believe him, Mort, so does Dixon. The fella seems genuine enough to me.'

Mort growled, 'The hell he is, Goddamnit! And as for Dixon . . . useless! I'll see he's out next election, if it takes every last dollar I got.'

Jim raised dark brows, shocked by the venom in Mort's tone.

'Easy, *amigo*, a man who don't play your game don't make him useless. Dixon came with an impressive record. Like it or not, right now we need him. I figure he's as good a lawman as we're going to get.'

The Slash B owner continued to glare.

'You do, uh? Well, we'll differ on that one, *compadre*,' he said. He waved a hand. 'Well, you'd better get some sleep; I'll have a man bury Mace out on the prairie before he starts to stink. What I recall, he's got no kin to notify. Am I right?'

'You're right,' Jim said.

*

Jim didn't know a thing until five in the morning when Mort rousted him out of his bunk. It felt like he'd never been to bed. Stripped to the waist, he sloshed the sleep off himself under the outside hand-pump gushing icy water. Then he dressed and ate breakfast in the bunkhouse. It proved to be a quiet affair. There was none of the usual cheerful banter and the men who had made up the Slash B posse for the past five days were yawning and bleary-eyed. Nevertheless, they ate heartily enough, as any hard-riding 'puncher, despite the odds, was known to do.

After breakfast Mort, though looking pale and worn, his eyes full of pain, detailed a man to ride into town and give Dixon the story. Then he picked out another groups of riders. Meanwhile, Jim gave the rest of the Slash B crew their work schedule for the next four days. He figured they might be out that long, going on how long it had taken the last time. However, he had a gut feeling – though no way did he like it – that once more this was going to be another frustrating and fruitless search. Nevertheless, on the other hand, they just might get lucky.

Quién sabe?

CHAPTER SEVENTEEN

They'd been at the lynching site ten minutes when Talbot Dixon rode up. He had six men behind him. The reason, he explained, was there wasn't the enthusiasm in town for the hunt a second time around. Most men had wives, families and businesses to run, he explained, and, in any case, most were plain doubtful about achieving any success after their failures over the past five days.

Jim found such lack of enthusiasm in the men disappointing. However, he also knew there was still bad feeling around town, chiefly because of the fact that Slash B had escaped punishment. Indeed, right now, he knew some people even felt that justice was being done through the selective killings of Slash B men known to have been in on the Cadman killings.

Interrupting his morbid thoughts, Buffalo Killer rode in. Mort must have sent him out while he had been asleep – to scout the hanging site? Judging by the broad grin on the Indian's face he'd picked up sign, and indeed he triumphantly announced that he had.

'Gottum, son of bitch!' he said.

The tracks took them into the north-eastern foothills. Again, up here, as Jim had fully expected, the rocky terrain made tracks difficult to detect and follow. To express his continued frustration he clamped lips together as tight as a gintrap and glowered around him. That bastard sure knew what he was doing when it came to shaking off a posse! The heat of the day was not helping: already two stops had been made to cool off and rest the horses.

Around six in the afternoon sign was again lost and Buffalo Killer moved on ahead to search. Meanwhile, the townspeople dismounted, generally pointing out it was no use going on while Buffalo Killer was seeking tracks. And, surprising Jim as well as Mort because there was at least another hour or more of passable daylight, Talbot Dixon acceded to their demands and decided to make night camp.

Mort roared furious objections. However, despite his vitriolic protests fires were built and supper was cooked and eaten. It was the end of an era, Jim realized. Mort Basset was no longer the giant figure he had been in Wild Horse Basin, but realization of that fact would not go down well at all with fiery Mort Basset, that was for sure.

An hour past sundown Buffalo Killer drifted in. He claimed the encroaching dark had beaten him, but declared he would ride out come dawn to continue the search. After his announcement he helped himself to a large helping of steak and eggs. Observing him, Mort growled.

'Damnation, go easy there, Injun; rations is limited.'

Buffalo Killer waved a dismissive hand. 'Not go short,

Basset. Buffalo Killer shoot deer, if go short.'

'Damned Injun,' grumbled Mort, then he grimaced and held his sore head. 'And damn this head all to hell!'

Jim looked into the last of the twilight. By now, the cold of night in these high places had closed in with a vengeance. The necessary chores done, the possemen were now huddled around the two big fires in order to keep warm. But Jim soon found out that, despite the men having full stomachs and being reasonably warm, there was still a deal of dissatisfaction amongst them, and it was Buffalo Killer who was the object of that large dose of that bitter discontent. However, it went no further than that . . . for the moment.

At 5.30 the next morning, while scarred enamel break-fast plates and cups were being washed in the chuckling stream beside which they were camped, Buffalo Killer returned. Being a member of a proud nation, he rode erect and triumph was written all over his swarthy, aquiline features. With his dark-brown eyes he picked out Mort.

'Found tracks,' he said.

'Damned time,' Mort growled. Then once again he groaned and held his head in both hands, moaning.

Jim looked keenly at his friend. Mort's face was even more grey and drawn this morning and his utterances regarding his pain were becoming more frequent and, worryingly, more slurred.

'You OK, *compadre*?' he asked.

Mort cut the air with a gnarled hand, clearly annoyed by the enquiry.

'I'll live, dammit. Let's get trailin'. We've wasted enough time.'

'As you say,' Jim said. Well, that was Mort.

119

The tracks led them south, along the back of the foothills and through the badlands, then back into the hills again. By noon Buffalo Killer had lost tracks again and was once more out quartering the broken ground. With nibbles of anger now gnawing at his gut, Jim became firmly of the opinion that either this was one very wily customer they were trying to run down, or the army had grossly exaggerated the tracking abilities of Buffalo Killer.

It was here that Jim felt more than a little guilt chewing at him, for he was himself no mean hand at finding sign, though he reluctantly accepted that he would probably be having the same difficulty as the Indian had it been he who was doing the trailing. Nevertheless. . . . He stared at Mort.

'Figure I should go out with Buffalo Killer, four eyes bein' better than two.'

Mort glared. 'To hell with that! What the hell d'you think I'm payin' the damned Injun for?'

'Mort, I'm makin' sense here,' Jim said. 'Git off your high horse.'

Mort glared, his face reddening. 'Leave it, y'hear me?'

'Damn you! Listen for once, will you?' Jim said.

He did not get any further. Mort made to bark a reply, then gasped and grabbed his head.

'Just leave it, Jim, will yuh?' he said quietly.

Jim opened his mouth to give a sharp answer, but held his peace. He was beginning to feel real concern now for Mort's condition. No way could this continued pain his *amigo* was suffering be right. He would have to get a sawbones in who knew about treating sore heads. Mort was no longer the stone-hard, gut-determined, bull-headed man he had known for twenty-five years. Right now, he was a very sick man.

By sundown it was clear that the posse's collective frustration was at breaking point. As they sat eating supper, Jim met Mort's pain-racked gaze as it reached for him across the plate of bacon and beans his friend was picking at.

'Coming to the opinion that damned Injun ain't worth a plugged nickel,' Mort said.

'I offered to go out,' Jim said.

Mort sighed. 'Yeah; guess my refusing was a mistake.' He stared. 'Go out with him in the morning, Jim, an' shake up his damned Cheyenne hide.'

Jim stared. Mort Basset admitting he'd been wrong? He frowned.

'You OK, Mort?' he asked.

Mort glared. 'Damn it! You my nursemaid now?' Then he emitted a pain-stricken, 'Hah!', grimaced and groaned and clasped the top of his Stetson. 'Damned head! Damn! Damn! Damn!'

Seriously concerned now, Jim said, 'Mort, calm down, this bawlin' ain't doin' you any good.'

Mort glared while grimacing at the same time.

'Will yah leave it?'

Then came the familiar bark of that god-awful rifle once more, booming noise into the black night. Startled, Jim felt his gut clench up, the beans and bacon he was chewing on forgotten. Worse, Frank Lawson, who was seated next to him, let out a grunt as he was driven back by the force of the bullet hitting him.

Jim dropped flat and stared at Lawson's face, not inches from his. He saw there was a bloody hole about half an inch above the top of Frank's nose and that gore, pieces of skull and brains were leaking out of the larger hole that had been blown out of the back of Frank's head. Frank's grey eyes now stared vacantly into the star-and-moonlit infinity above, his half-eaten plate of beans and bacon now spilled out of his lifeless hands and on to his lap. Jim knew Frank was dead before his back hit the grass. Meantime, Mort was roaring, his pain apparently forgotten.

'Will somebody kill those damned fires?'

The demand was not needed where Jim was concerned. Already, he was scrambling to his feet, and moments later he was kicking out both fires while drawing his Colt .45. When the fires were just scattered embers he dived into the cover of the nearby brush. Once there he glared into the night. As soon as that big rifle boomed he had the flash from it located . . . out there in that black beyond.

Driven by pure frustration he sent five slugs towards where that vivid spurt of fire had showed, even though he knew that that son of a bitch was well out of the range of his handgun. However, he was satisfied to hear that his was not the only weapon blazing away. Several guns were now whacking noise into the night, their harsh echoes chasing each other away into the dark, looming bulks of the hills.

Jim was reloading when he observed Buffalo Killer slip off into the night. Pursuing the bushwhacker? He went after him, crouched Indian style and ignoring the scratches he received from the sharp twigs of the brush he was crawling through. Seconds later he caught up with the eagle-faced Indian. Frustratingly, he also heard the thud of a horse's hoofs pounding away out there.

A guttural Cheyenne expletive issued from Buffalo Killer's lips.

'Him son of bitch!' he said. He reared up, pulled his

Winchester into his shoulder and jacked off three shots. Their echoes quarrelled into the dark night. Moments later Talbot Dixon came crashing out of the brush, his long gun clasped in his right hand.

'You git him?' he said.

Jim said, 'In this dark?'

The hoofbeats were swiftly fading into the darkness. Nevertheless, clearly driven by frustration, Buffalo Killer and Dixon sent hot lead hissing into the night until no more hoofbeats could be heard.

The two finally lowered their rifles and Dixon said with raw feeling,

'Damn that no good son of a bitch!' He turned and Jim met his stare as the lawman said, in a totally different, even soft, tone,

'I regret to tell you this, Alston, but Frank Lawson is dead.'

Jim nodded. 'Know it. I was right next to him when he got it. But thanks anyway.'

'No thanks needed,' Dixon said. 'However, there is this other thing: reckon Lawson's demise means that only Bowdy Gleason, Mort and yourself are left alive out of the bunch that did for the Cadman clan.'

Jim stared. 'You can't let it go, can you?'

Dixon shook his head. 'No, sir,' he said. 'However, I repeat, being the law in this territory, it is my duty to catch the man we're chasin' and bring him to justice. But I guess it has been a kind of rough justice we've been witnessing over the last week or so.'

Jim's anger flared. 'Damn you, Dixon,' he said, 'I repeat: we were all cleared of any wrongdoing in a court of law.'

Dixon nodded. 'Yeah, that you were,' he said, 'and by twelve good men and true, no less.' He did not try to hide his cynicism.

'So live with it,' Jim snapped.

'Not my way,' said Dixon, 'and won't be until corruption and wrongdoing is a thing of the past in this territory.'

'An' y'all think I don't want that?' Jim said.

Dixon's grey-eyed scrutiny was thorough. Then he said, 'In a strange kind of way I think mebbe you do.'

Jim's thin lips curled into a sneer. 'Well, thank you for that,' he said bitterly, then he added, 'So, what you goin' to do about that murderin' son of a bitch out yonder, uh? Seein' as you're such a high-minded protector of the law.'

Dixon pursed his lips. 'He's got to slip up sometime,' he said, 'and when he does we'll have him. However,' he added, 'there'll be no more vigilante justice or bribed juries. That shooter will be brought in to face a *genuine* court of law. The outcome of that Broken Mesa fiasco has caused quite a stir in the territory, and rumour has it that Judge Neilson will be stripped of his job pretty soon.'

'Well, is that so?' Jim sneered. 'We'll see what happens on the day, uh?'

Dixon's hawklike expression set into deep, serious lines.

'Heed me, Jim,' he said, 'and pass the message on to your boss and the rest of the Slash B crew: no more vigilante justice. You hearin' me?'

Jim was about to answer when Buffalo Killer said, as if he had been removed from the conversation and thinking his own thoughts,

'I think I hit him, Dix-on. Heard him make "hurt"

noise. But could be horse making sound.'

The lawman stared through the starlit dark at the tall Indian.

'You sure about that?'

'I got good feeling,' the Cheyenne replied. 'Maybe now hit will slow him down. Catch him soon, maybe. Ugh!'

'*Maybe*'s the word.' Dixon said bitterly. Then he sighed heavily. 'Well, we'd better get back. Doin' no good here.'

When they hit camp Mort was rolling on the ground, obviously in great pain. All the Slash B men were standing round him, looking worried and clearly wondering what they could do to help.

Jim went down on to one knee beside Mort. His friend was definitely in a bad way.

'Dammit!' he said, his voice made harsh by his concern. 'We've got to get you to a doctor knows what he's doin', y'hear? You can't go on like this.'

Mort stared back, his blue eyes pleading, even appearing a little scared.

'These headaches, Jim, they ain't goin' away,' he said. Tiredly, he climbed to his feet and produced a small brown bottle from which he took a swig. He grimaced.

'Groddamn! Like drinkin' lion piss. Laudanum: supposed to help ease the pain. Truth is, I reckon that sawbones in Broken Mesa don't know what the hell he's doin'.'

'Told you, you should have stayed at the ranch and rested,' Jim said. 'You jest don't listen, do you?'

Mort scowled but, apparently feeling better, said, 'Well, to hell with *that*! I want that son of a bitch killed and I want to be there when it happens. I got five good men dead and you know that don't sit easy with me. By God, I'll see that bastard hang if it's the last thing I do.'

'He'll face a court of law, Basset,' Dixon said, 'not the end of a Slash B lych rope. And I've told your straw boss that too.'

Fury flashed red into Mort's pain-paled face.

'Damn your hide, Dixon! Don't you threaten me. Not ever.'

The lawman leaned forwards, menace in his look.

'I'll do more than that, Basset,' he said, 'and your smart lawyers won't help you next time.'

Mort glared and sneered. 'Can't take losin', can you?'

Dixon's stare was ice cold. 'Not where the law's concerned.'

'The Injun thinks he hit him,' Jim said to divert the brewing argument.

Mort turned to the Cheyenne. 'How d'you know?' he asked.

'I hear "hurt" noise,' Buffalo Killer said. 'That tell me.'

Mort scowled. '*Hurt* noise,' he said. 'What the hell's that supposed to mean? More of your damned Injun bullshit?'

'Not shit.' Buffalo Killer raised his right arm and waved the Winchester in his right hand. 'Hurt him, with this. Wagh!'

Mort glowered through the starlight at the triumphant Cheyenne and shook his head.

'Nothin' but a damned crazy Injun' he said, and then spat his contempt into the last glowing ashes of the nearest stamped-out campfire. It hissed and spluttered because of the heat still in it. Then Jim met his stare as he added, 'Sent a man back to Slash B with Lawson's body. He got kin?'

Jim nodded. 'Yes.'

'See they're informed,' Mort said.

'Goes without sayin',' Jim told him.

CHAPTER EIGHTEEN

Six o'clock the next morning, along with Buffalo Killer, Jim found tracks. There was also blood, a dry black trail of it. Jim informed Mort of the fact when they returned to camp. Mort spat brown juice.

'Well, seems the damned Injun was right after all,' he grudgingly admitted.

Jim tried not to grin because Mort always found it very hard to admit he was wrong.

'Yup, sure appears that way,' he said.

'That old cuss Bowdy Gleason rode out last night, maybe because of these killin's,' Mort said. 'I figure he won't be back.'

'That leaves just you an' me now, uh, *amigo*?' Jim queried.

Mort's stare was hard. 'Yeah, but we'll handle it,' he said. 'That son of a bitch has got to slip up sometime, and when he does we'll have him.'

Following the killer's tracks they topped the north-west ridge of the basin. From this high point Jim looked down on the Triple H ranch. It stood a mile down the bottom of a long grassy slope. Beeves were grazing contentedly.

Charlie Hathaway owned this small outfit, Jim knew and, to his surprise – mingled with suspicion – he saw that the tracks they followed led down to the ranch. Straight away he figured that to be mighty odd. Charlie Hathaway was a cowman through and through.

Followed by Mort and the posse, Jim urged his horse down the long slope and pulled rein before the modest pine-bole-constructed ranch house with its roof of warping shingles. A small bunkhouse was situated a hundred yards east; close to it was a corral that at present had five horses penned in it. Close by the corral was a medium-sized barn. A double clapboard-earth john was situated maybe a hundred yards away from the house and downwind.

'Charlie!' Mort called.

Hathaway appeared at the ranch house door. He was a solid-looking man of medium height, maybe five foot six, with a large bushy grey moustache and round amber eyes. He beamed a smile.

'Well, lookit here . . . Mort Basset . . . Jim Alston,' he said. He was clearly pleased. 'You're strangers hereabouts.'

'It's been some time, Charlie,' Jim said, 'we got to say.'

'You hear anybody passin' last night, Charlie?' Mort asked, as usual coming straight to the point.

'Now you come to mention it,' Charlie replied, 'we did have a visitor.' He led them to the corral and pointed. 'See the chestnut with the wound in its rump?'

Jim looked at the long, sore-looking gash, around which the horse's skin kept twitching, no doubt because of the soreness and the pestering flies. It had clearly been treated with some kind of unction, for it wasn't bleeding now.

'What about it?' Jim asked, but he half-guessed.

'Son of a bitch left that and took one of my best geldings,' Charlie said. 'Mind, that there is a fine quarter horse. Don't see many of them around here, so I ain't about to complain too much.'

'Didn't you hear him?' Mort asked.

Charlie shook his head. 'Nary a sound. If we had my two sons and me would've given chase.' He waved a hand. 'We know these hills inside out,' he boasted.

'You hear about my boys gettin' killed?' Mort wanted to know.

Hathaway stared for moments. A frown formed on his brow, then he shook his head.

'Can't say I have,' he answered. 'Unless somebody's passing we don't get much news out here. Have to go into town and we haven't done *that* in a fortnight – been kind of busy.' As if the news was only just now sinking in he added, 'Did you say you've had some hands *killed?*'

Mort was about to answer when he gasped, held his head and swayed in the saddle as if dazed.

'Oh! Jesus!' he said. Jim saw sweat beading his brow. With a shaking hand Mort lifted out the brown laudanum bottle, took a dose and again grimaced at its clearly foul taste. After some seconds, after the laudanum had taken effect, he said,

'Yup, that's what I said.' He named the dead men and then explained why his head was bandaged. Charlie Hathaway's look was one of awe.

'The hell you say?'

Mort nodded. 'I do,' he said firmly.

He returned the brown medicine bottle to his coat pocket. Then he went on:

'Feel like doing some riding, Charlie, knowing this part of the territory like you do?' He waved a calloused hand in Buffalo Killer's direction. 'We haven't had a deal of luck with this damned Injun doin' the trailin'.'

The Cheyenne stiffened and gripped his Winchester until his knuckles turned white. Raw resentment filtered into his brown eyes, then he said,

'Taken bad talk from Bas-set long enough. I go now. Not come back.'

Mort appeared to look surprised. 'Ain't you gone yet?' he jeered.

'Son of bitch!' Buffalo Killer exploded. 'You owe me ten dollar!'

'Is that right?' Mort said. 'Well, don't want a man to say I don't pay my debts.' He pulled a leather purse from the inside pocket of his coat. He counted out silver and gave it to the Cheyenne. 'Now git your ass outa here.'

Buffalo Killer's stare was malicious.

'Watch *your* ass, white man,' he said. With that he pulled his pinto around and kicked its flanks. Turf flew up from the beast's hoofs as it took off.

Mort reached for his Colt.

'Did he threaten me?' he demanded of Jim, but gave him no time to reply as he called after the Indian, 'Why, you red son of a bitch, I'll—'

Mort stiffened, but did not lift his weapon. Instead, he began to shake violently and Jim saw that blood was now trickling out of his friend's right ear. He saw too that Mort's face was ashen, and that those once ruddy but now sallow features held a look of bewilderment as he groaned.

'Goddamn it! The hell's the matter with me?'

Again he pulled out his bottle of laudanum and took a

131

big gulp.

'Easy with that stuff,' Dixon said.

Mort glared. 'You talkin' to me, lawman?'

Dixon shrugged, his look indifferent.

'Go ahead; poison yourself,' he said. 'Ain't no skin off my hide.'

'About ridin' with you, Mort,' Charlie Hathaway said, as if to change the subject. 'No problem at all. I'll welcome the change. I'll get saddled up.' He turned to the house and called, 'Molly!'

Charlie was well known in the basin for his steadfast nature and, in the earlier days, his capable tracking abilities when Kiowa Indians or marauding Long Riders visited the basin to kill, steal beeves and cause all sorts of mayhem.

Raw-boned and formidable-looking, Molly Hathaway came to the door, wiping flour off her hands.

'You want somethin', Charlie?' she asked. She glanced around. 'Howdy, Mort . . . Jim? Yo'se strangers hereabouts.'

Courteously, Mort touched his hat. 'Molly. Allus good to see you.'

'Likewise,' Jim added. 'You're still a fine-lookin' lady, Molly, I got to say.'

Molly beamed a smile. 'Why, thank you, Jim Alston,' she said, 'an' I got to say you're still a fine-lookin' man!'

Jim grinned mischievously. 'Can't argue with that.'

'Ridin' with Mort fer a while, Molly,' Charlie said. 'I'll leave a note for the boys.'

Jim knew Charlie had two strapping sons whom he worked really hard. Charlie turned to Mort and explained.

'Boys are down Blake's Canyon looking for strays.'

Mort nodded approvingly. 'You're right to keep 'em at it, Charlie,' he said.

'Will you be needin' vittles, husband?' asked Molly.

'We got enough, Molly,' Mort told her, then he gazed at the Triple H owner. 'Really appreciate this, Charlie, you know that.'

However, Jim could see that sweat was running down Mort's face, and it wasn't the heat. It was clear that Mort was really in bad pain but was bearing it manfully. Well, that was Mort.

Out from the ranch a piece now it wasn't long before Charlie fastened on to tracks that he said weren't his or his boys'. By noon-break Jim felt they were getting somewhere when they found a camp that had clearly been used the night before, and by one person.

Jim sharpened up his gaze, his gut tightening as he searched the pleasant open country around them. This was perfect sniping country. However, the day progressed without incident. On the second day out after leaving the Triple H Jim couldn't help but curse. They had lost tracks again.

'One hell of a tricky customer,' a disheartened Charlie Hathaway said. He had just returned from searching the high country, while Jim had explored this scrub-strewn lower ground.

'You can say that agin,' Jim said bitterly.

'An' I got to confess,' Charlie went on, 'he's got me beat.'

Jim stared. 'Never figured to hear Charlie Hathaway say *that*.'

Charlie sighed, raised his slouch hat and scratched his

matted grey head, then shook his head.

'Mebbe I'm just gittin' too old and ain't realized it,' he said.

Mort snorted. 'Well that's a damn fine thing, I got to say!'

A town posseman, whom Jim knew to be ass-sore with riding and didn't mind who knew it, said,

'Knew from the start this'd be a damn waste of time.'

Mort glared. 'Git, if you can't stomach it,' he growled. Then his features twisted as if he had again been hit by sudden, acute pain. He clasped his head. 'Jesus H. Christ, this just ain't right . . . can't be.' He wobbled in the saddle and Jim saw his eyeballs roll up until they showed only white before his body seemed to melt and lose all muscular control.

Mort fell out of the saddle and hit the ground hard.

Jim dismounted along with Dixon. Each of them went down on one knee by Mort's side. His eyes, pupils dilated, were staring straight up at the blue sky. They were blood-shot, looking as though Mort had been on a fortnight's drunken jag. There was also what looked like bad bruising pouched under each eye, and blood was again running from his ear, as well as his nose. Jesus! Anxiously, Jim felt for the pulse in Mort's wrist, as he had often seen saw-bones do, and found Mort's heart was still beating, but faintly.

'Well?' Dixon asked.

'He's livin',' Jim told him. 'Just.'

Charlie Hathaway came down on the other side of Mort.

'By the looks of him we need to build a travois,' he said. 'Get him down to the ranch; send for a doctor.'

But not one of the posse men climbed down. Clearly nervous, they were staring anxiously at the ambush country around them. Jim ignored them for now, his concern for Mort paramount.

'That makes a deal of sense to me, Charlie,' he said. He glared up at the mounted men and added, 'Damn glad somebody's thinkin' here.'

'Hell, Jim,' a posseman complained, 'that son of a bitch out there could be pointin' a rifle at us right now. We got to keep a lookout.'

'He ain't within miles of us!' said Jim. 'Me an' Charlie here would've known if he was.'

'So you say,' the posseman said, clearly unconvinced.

Jim glared. 'You want to be useful – uh – uh? Well, git down to Triple H and warn them we're comin'. Tell 'em Mort's real sick. Molly'll know what to do.'

As if happy to be doing something to get himself out of what he plainly figured was a death trap, the man replied, 'On my way.'

Damned right you are, thought Jim with disgust.

The posseman dug his heels in and his chestnut gelding kicked up dirt and dust as he headed the beast down the narrow valley. Jim stared around at the rest of the men.

'Cut wood; let's get a travois built.'

Less than half an hour later the makeshift travois was constructed and the unconscious Mort was secured on to it.

By mid-afternoon they arrived at the Triple H. Two men carried the still comatose Mort into the bedroom that the capable Molly Hathaway must have prepared. The redoubtable Molly bustled along behind them, a worried look fixed on her hard face.

Moon Child, her Paiute maid, was bustling along beside her. Jim knew the small, plump-faced Indian woman had been with the Hathaway family since she was a child, having been abandoned when her parents fled from a revenge raid on their camp after four ranch hands had been slaughtered in a Paiute horse raid. Jim was relieved to learn that a rider was on his way to Broken Mesa to get the sawbones.

Jim watched as with female efficiency the two women stripped Mort down to his long johns and pulled blankets over him. Then they sat, patiently cooling his brow with cloths dipped in cold water.

Knowing Mort was in good hands, Jim quietly left the bedroom.

An hour later, when all the possemen were settled down to a meal, sitting with their backs against the wall of the small Triple H barn, Deputy Sheriff George Smith rode down the hill and into the ranch precincts. His big piebald was sweat-lathered. Frowning, Talbot Dixon rose and went out to meet him. Jim followed.

George climbed down stiffly and ground-hitched his mount. His serious gaze met Dixon's grey eyes.

'A real bad killing out at Triple Forks, Talbot,' he said. 'Fred Madison's been back-shot. Rumour is the mayor's son is responsible. Mayor denies it, of course, and wants to know where you are. Guess you'd better come or there'll be hell to pay. He has big friends.'

Jim's gut tightened. Deputy Sheriff Fred Madison? Shot? He watched Dixon's steely stare harden.

'The hell you say!' the lawman exclaimed. He stood rubbing his chin, then he turned. Jim met his stare.

'The ball's in your court, Alston,' Dixon said. 'Got to look into this.'

'Will you be leavin' George here?'

Dixon shook his head. 'Not a chance; I need him in town.'

Jim found that that reply did not cause him overmuch concern. Maybe, even, it would allow him to move more freely, without constantly having to consider whether the moves he had in mind were lawful.

One of the possemen rose to his feet. His face was drawn; three days' growth of beard shadowed his features.

'I figure to ride with the sheriff,' he said. 'Ain't doin' no good here. That son of a bitch is long gone.'

At this announcement the rest of the townsmen rose. One of them looked around him.

'Likewise, huh, boys?'

His suggestion was was met with nods of agreement and Jim found he had to concede: there had been nothing but dead ends all the way. For sure, that bastard out there had run them ragged, though Jim personally found that difficult to admit to. Five minutes later Sheriff Talbot Dixon and Deputy George Smith, who now forked a fresh horse, and the whole bunch of townsmen were riding out. Jim compressed his lips. Though he was pleased in one way, the whole thing was still a mess.

He glared at the distant ridges rising above the Triple H. His thoughts were wholly on the killer: *You're out there somewhere, damn you, and by God if it's the last thing I do, I'll find you.*

He turned to the Slash B riders. They were still sitting with their backs resting against Charlie's barn. Some were whittling, some were still eating, but all looked concerned for, as Jim well knew, despite his many faults, Mort was still held in high esteem by those men. They clearly did not want him to die.

Jim found that his mind was working hard. There was a possibility, with Howdy Gleason decamping during last night, that that son of a bitch out there was thinking his work was done and he could relax. He might even get a little careless. And that, thought Jim, could prove a bad mistake.

He found hope was building up in him. Yes: perhaps that smart ass was thinking he had wreaked enough vengeance with five men dead and one on the run, and Mort Basset gravely ill in the house behind, maybe even dying. But there was one mystery: why did that sidewinder out there leave Jim Alston alive? Was it because he knew Jim Alston had tried to stop the killings and he was honouring that attempt by letting him live? That wasn't likely, or was it?

He stared at the men leaning against the barn. After recent neglect there must be a lot of work waiting to be done at Slash B. Best thing to do was send the boys back. Billy Carlson – that bright young fellow he'd taken under his wing recently – knew how to handle the *segundo*'s job. Indeed, he had been handling things while Mort and he had been out chasing that no-good killer. Billy would know what work needed to be done around the ranch and would be getting it seen to. The decision came quickly.

'Get back to the ranch, boys,' Jim said. 'Billy Carlson will hand out your work until Mort an' me get back.'

Looking surprised, all the men got to their feet and dusted themselves down.

'How about that killer out there, Jim? asked Bowleg

Jimmy Hayes.

'I'll deal with him. Been figurin'; one man might not raise as much dust as twenty an' that'll give me the edge that's mebbe been lackin'.'

'It's a possibility,' Bowleg said, but dubiously.

Jim nodded. 'It is,' he said more positively. 'Now git while you've still got good light.'

He watched the men head off. Then he went back into the house and pulled up a chair so he could sit with Mort.

Relieved to be free to do the chores needed to keep even a small ranch running smoothly, Molly Hathaway nevertheless brought in thick, steaming hot black coffee, which Jim sipped gratefully. Jim knew that Moon Child, the Paiute, was already busy in the kitchen. But the fact remained: Mort had not recovered consciousness yet, and that was a real worry.

CHAPTER NINETEEN

Mort died during the night. He had not recovered consciousness. Now, filled with almost overpowering grief, Jim tied Mort on to the back of his horse, said goodbye to Charlie Hathaway and Molly, who promised to follow on shortly so they could be present at the burial, then took his long-time friend back to Slash B.

Doc Sumner said he thought Mort had probably died of a brain haemorrhage; he wanted to open him up to find out. Jim told him he could not allow that. Mort Basset would be buried a whole man.

Three days later Mort was interred on the hill overlooking the spread they had both, by the sweat of their brows, accuracy of their aim and with pure guts and determination fought for and built up to become the largest ranch in the territory.

Looking around, Jim reckoned there must have been over a hundred people present as Pastor Hannibal Griffiths boomed his moving eulogy over the heads-bowed mourners.

When they had all gone Dolly Grover stayed with Jim, saying she just did not know what were the best words to comfort him. While he drank whiskey, taking little food with it, she just sat patiently with him on the veranda – or wherever he happened to be at the time – and, with sympathy, held his calloused hand.

Jim stayed drunk for a whole week. But in the second week, with him still drinking, Molly lost her temper and slapped his face real hard.

'Damn you, Jim Alston, will you quit?' she shouted.

Shocked, bleary-eyed and rubbing his cheek, he stared at her.

'What the hell?'

He looked around. He observed that he was lying on the veranda's boards, an empty bottle in his hand. He must have drunk himself into oblivion . . . again.

'What day is it?' he slurred.

'You been out of it more'n a week, goddamn it!' Molly said.

Jim blinked, as though seeing daylight for the first time in God knew how long.

'That right?' he said. 'Who's lookin' after things?'

'Damn you! Billy Carlson. Who d'you think?' fumed Molly.

With a struggle Jim got to his feet and stood swaying and shaking his head. Then he said, as if seeing her for he first time,

'Molly, honey, what are you doin' here? Ain't you got a steakhouse to run?'

Her kick landed on his right shin and sent him hopping down the veranda, howling his pain. Then he stopped and, clearly hurt by such physical abuse and rubbing his bruised shin, he said, as if bewildered,

'What yuh done that for?'

141

Molly glared. 'Just for the hell of it! What d'you think? You worryin' me to death like you done!'

She stomped off the veranda down the three steps, and said over her shoulder,

'I'll be in town if you ever get sober enough to visit.'

Becoming more cognizant by the second Jim called, 'Now hold on here, Molly. I need you!'

She stopped halfway across the patch of bare ground in front of the ranch house. Rage flashed in her bright green eyes.

'*You* need *me*? What *you* need is a good kick in the ass,' she said. 'Jim, that no-good son of a bitch Basset is dead and no amount of drinkin' is goin' to bring him back. Get it through your head.'

' 'Tain't as easy as that,' he protested.

'Make it so,' she shouted.

Head thumping like a drum being beaten in an echoing cave Jim stared after her. He was still swaying-drunk and clinging to the veranda rail for support when, five minutes later, she galloped out of the bigger barn of the two, glared at him as she rode past and then urged her chestnut into a drumming run. Soon she was just a dot in a faint trail of dust on the horizon.

Making it worse, those hands who were working around the ranch house had stopped to grin at him. Furious at seeing those leers he glared and roared,

'The hell's the matter with you? Ain't you got work to do?'

Sick to his stomach he flopped into the nearest of the wicker chairs. His anger faded and his grief drifted in again with gut-wrenching force.

Mort was gone, never to return. What was he to do?

Mort had been the driving force throughout – always doing the thinking, the scheming, the figuring, and Jim Alston had been the faithful friend at his side and had gone along with his plans . . . most of the time, anyway. Once more, he felt hot drunken tears course down his range-worn. deep-tanned features. Though he fought the effects of drink still working on him he again sank into morbid alcohol-driven oblivion.

It was silver dark when he woke up. The moon was full and overhead and the stars were a vast spread of diamonds across the deep-purple sky. He looked around. The ranch and its environs were as quiet as a tomb, as it should be at this time of night. He licked his lips. His mouth had the taste of God knew what. For sure, whatever it was it wasn't pleasant.

He groaned, wobbled off the veranda, put his head under the water pump and started working the lever. The ice-cold water shocked him to full wakefulness, but he still held his head under and also gulped water until the fog caused by his crazy days spent drinking gradually cleared and he began to think rationally again. God, what a bastard he had been with Molly. Even so, it wasn't long before the killing of five Slash B men and the death of Mort took full precedence in his mind, as well as Bowdy Gleason, who had hightailed it. Couldn't blame the man. But, strangely, again he had this feeling that the killing was now over; that the killer had satisfied his need for revenge. Because of that it was a big possibility that he would maybe never get to know who that man was. Indeed, it could be any one of the dozen or so sodbusters in the area . . . or relatives he did not know about.

It could even be Luke Freeman. The man most certainly had cause.

Jim remembered, however, that Freeman had claimed to be a man of God and so he could not kill, and that he had three young children to feed, clothe, love and teach. Truth be known, brooded Jim, Freeman came over as a man who only lived by the truth, so how *could* it be him? Even so, Freeman had also seen John Cadman hanged and watched Jane Cadman and her children fry and that could do all kinds of crazy things to a man. Jim halted his thoughts.

Fry?

What was he doing using such a pitiless word in that context? The Cadman woman and her children had been murdered, and in the most horrific way. Worst of all, Jim Alston had been part of that horror, despite doing his damnedest to stop it happening. The whole thing had been a terrible blunder and his best friend had been the instigator of that disaster. He had paid the price but had taken five – what you could call – less blameworthy men down with him. To Jim Alston's way of thinking, that was a real sadness.

Jim walked out on to the range. A coyote yipped over by the bluffs; wolves howled on the wooded ridges, a cougar screamed. The whole world was a killing zone when you came to think about it, he brooded, and he was still considering adding to the killing. But the act of revenge did not seem to be the answer any more. Revenge had already killed five men and caused Jim Alston to suffer the loss of the best friend a man could ever have. And – how could he forget? – that was not counting the anguish the deaths of the Cadman family caused the Freeman family to suffer, and the subsequent revenge that followed those awful killings.

Jim slowed his thoughts as a startling decision suddenly invaded his morbid thinking: *hard as it would be to do it, he must let this go.* There must be no more killings, no more blood spilt. It was over. Let it go. Nevertheless, this need to know still burnt like a bright flame deep within him; this urge to know the man they had tracked for so long without success; the man who was responsible for the killing of so many Slash B men, rightly or wrongly. In a strange, grudging, even crazy way, Jim could not help but admire the fellow and the way he applied his own primitive punishment for the terrible and murderous injustices inflicted upon the completely innocent Cadman family.

But damn you, Mort Basset, for being the cause of it all!

Nevertheless, the intense curiosity to know still gnawed like a ravenous wolf at his gut.

CHAPTER TWENTY

The ride to Cheyenne took close to a week. When Jim came out of the marshal's office, achieving the end of a ride over a wide area of territory seeking information that had swallowed up another fortnight, he was a man full of amazement.

Could Maureen Freeman really be *the* person? It was repeatedly asserted by the locals that at one time Maureen Freeman, née Bridges, was renowned in the area for her deadly accuracy with a long gun, and that she had won every competition she entered.

In particular, she had revelled in going up against the buffalo hunters who swarmed all over the territory. They were renowned for the accuracy of their long-distance shooting and were more than garrulous about their ability to outshoot all comers.

Nine times out of ten, it was reported, she out-shot the hide off all of them and then gleefully walked away with the prize money. On top of that, she was also known for her more than capable tracking abilities, having been taught by her grizzled uncle, the renowned and highly respected ex-mountain man, Jedidiah Bridges. That disclosure produced another story: of how Jedidiah had come into her life.

The story went that there had been a terrible occurrence during the Civil War in which her parents had been blown to bits by a badly directed Union mortar shell. Worse, the four very young children who survived would have probably been left to fend for themselves, or been taken into dubious care, had not uncle Jedidiah Bridges got to know of the tragedy and broken off scouting for General 'Hard Backsides' Custer, as the Crow Indians called him, to take action.

He undertook to rear four-year-old Maureen, apparently his favourite, and then had sent the three remaining children – two brothers and a sister – to be brought up by relatives living in Philadelphia.

But the matter of most interest to Jim in his probing was the fact that Maureen Freeman had never been back to Cheyenne, as her husband Luke Freedman had claimed.

Indeed, according to local information, she had ridden out of Cheyenne six years ago and nobody had seen hide or hair of her since. Jedidiah Bridges, now a gnarled teller of tall tales about his hair-raising mountain man adventures to anybody who would buy him a drink and take the time to listen, was mighty curious to know as much about her as Jim Alston was able to tell. In fact, Jedidiah, when Jim asked him if he knew of her whereabouts, pretty nearly demanded to know how she was getting along these days.

Mainly he wanted to know whether she was still the feisty girl he had reared, despite her getting strong religion and going off like she did to seek the right Christian man and find a place with more in-depth piety than was to

147

be found here in ungodly Cheyenne.

Jim could only assure the old man that she was getting along fine far as he knew and was still dutifully and piously going along to church every Sunday with her family.

Now, five weeks later, back on home range, on a hill over-looking the Freeman homestead, Jim chewed on his lower lip. He watched Maureen playing with her three children, out on the recently mown grass meadow.

Could she really be the revenge seeker, the executioner, the super-competent person they'd found impossible to run down?

Jim found the idea took some hard believing. Did her husband know about her unwomanly activities? Had he been lying through his teeth to protect her?

Jim shook his head. Dammit, no, she was a *woman*; women did not do such things, particularly if they were now as devout as Jedidiah Bridges made her out to be.

Nevertheless, with the information he now possessed, Jim felt compelled, though strangely, and with a deal of reluctance, to accept that Maureen Freeman was indeed able to do all those vengeful things that had been done: that she must be the perpetrator.

He shook his head. His mind was now a battleground of indecision. In his heart of hearts he wanted to bury the whole business, wash his hands of it. But the old saying now bounced around in his brain: *an eye for an eye, a tooth for a tooth.* Damn it, this thing just would not go away.

Movement to the left dragged him out of his musings and he observed Sheriff Talbot Dixon riding in on the Broken Mesa trail, toward the Freeman homestead. He saw that the children and Maureen Freeman, who had obviously seen him too, were now heading back to the homestead. On reaching it they stood outside to await the sheriff's arrival.

There was no sign of her husband, Luke Freeman, and Jim found that odd. Why that should be he couldn't rationally answer right now, except to recall that when he'd spoken with the man previously he had seemed very protective.

Dixon reined up before cabin. An animated discussion began to take place between the woman and Dixon. Intensely curious now, Jim urged his roan down the hill and took an out-of-sight roundabout route to reach the Broken Mesa trail. On reaching it he selected a clump of brush to hide behind, climbed down, and waited for Dixon to finish talking with Maureen.

He rolled a quirly and was lighting it when he saw granger Luke Freeman come out of the trees half a mile to the north. With long stride he walked towards the homestead. He carried a small, obviously dead deer across his shoulders and his Springfield single-shot rifle, Jim noted, was grasped firmly in his right hand. Was it a remnant of his service in the Civil War? Maybe.

Freeman joined his wife and children. Carefully, he lowered the deer he was carrying to the ground and then he stared at Dixon. Talk started between the two men; some of it clearly hostile. However, after five minutes or so had passed the lawman nodded, touched the brim of his low-crowned grey hat and turned his mount. He guided it on to the Broken Mesa trail, where he kicked flanks and headed for home.

Jim extinguished what remained of his quirly, mounted, and waited for the lawman's arrival. Dixon clearly saw him long before he reached him. As he closed up the lawman's gaze became as hard as Toledo steel.

'The hell you want, Alston?' he demanded.

'Maybe to chat with Mrs Freeman a while.'

'About where she's been the past month?' Dixon asked.

Jim nodded. 'Uh-uh.'

Dixon stared, then said, 'Philadelphia She's been to Philadelphia. She has kin there. That enough?'

Jim nodded again. 'Uh-huh. Maybe. Anything else?'

Dixon stared. 'What else is there? Grievin' is what; that was what she went there to do.'

Jim raised an eyebrow. 'An' that's it?'

Dixon nodded. 'That's it. By the way, I got news for you. There's a New York lawyer in town. He wants to talk to you.'

'About?'

'Didn't ask. Ain't my business.'

Dixon urged his horse forward and Jim dug in heels to catch up. He wasn't through with Dixon yet.

'You got me curious,' he said, matching his horse's gait to Dixon's.

'About what?' Dixon said.

'Mrs Freeman,' Jim said. 'Is that all you talked about? Grievin'?'

'One or two other things; no concern of yours.'

'With six Slash B men dead it has to be my concern.'

Dixon eased up his horse, and gazed keenly at Jim. 'You figure she had somethin' to do with that?'

'Leave nothin' out. Ain't that your motto?'

The steel remained in Dixon's stare.

'You're forgettin' somethin',' he said. 'What about Cadman ... dead; his woman and children ... dead, burnt; don't those murders count?'

Jim found that these remarks made him exceedingly uncomfortable; however, he said,

'Not the same, dammit.'

'No,' Dixon cut in, 'the Cadman business was worse. Mean, cowardly, and vicious in the extreme. Slash B, in my opinion, got all it deserved.' He leaned forward, his look grim. 'And what's more, Alston, you know it.'

Dixon now eased back into the saddle. He stared at Jim for some moments, then urged his horse on again.

'Leave it, Alston, you hear me?'

'You know she has kin in Cheyenne?' Jim called after him.

'I do.'

'You checked up on that?'

'I did.'

'And?'

'Nothin',' snapped Dixon. 'It's over, done with. Get it through your head.'

Dixon spurred his mount into a gallop. Jim had to urge his horse hard to keep up with him. But though Jim tried to draw him out, Dixon would not enlarge on what he had already said.

At the livery stable at the top of Broad Street Dixon left his horse and walked the boardwalk to his office. As he reached it he turned and stared at Jim.

'Go see your lawyer, Alston,' he said. 'Maybe you've just inherited a ranch to run.' Then he turned and slammed the office door shut.

Jim sought out the lawyer Dixon had referred to. He found him at the Rangeman's Rest hotel on Broad Street He was Mr John Chadwick and was in room 10. Jim knocked on the door. The man who opened it was tall, well built, with dark hair and a thick nicotine-browned moustache. His blue-grey eyes were arresting.

'Yes?' he said. 'Mr Jim Alston?'

'On the button,' Jim said. 'Bin told you want to see me, Mr Chadwick.'

A smile exposed Chadwick's clean, healthy teeth.

'Yes, yes, come in.' He waved a hand and stood aside. Jim strolled in, taking off his old, dusty hat. He found he was full of expectation.

Chadwick shut the door, waved him into an easy chair and then sat in the other chair opposite him.

'What's this about, Mr Chadwick?' Jim asked.

Chadwick beamed. 'Straight to the point, I like that. It's about Mr Mort Basset's will, sir. The benefits you will receive.'

'It's all settled,' Jim said. 'Should he go first, Mort left the ranch an' all that goes with it to me when he lost his wife, two girls and three boys. Watched him make out the will in the lawyer's office, sign it – all settled, neat an' legal.'

Chadwick leaned back in the armchair, made a steeple with his fingers and said,

'Ah! Did he? Hum. Oh, dear. Well ... I'm afraid not quite *settled*, Mr Alston. There was a change made to the will, eighteen months ago. Did he not tell you?'

The hell there was, thought Jim. But then: Mort had made a long journey to New York about that time. Didn't tell him what it was about ... Jim felt something in his gut tighten up as he answered,

'No, he didn't.'

Chadwick cleared his throat. 'Hum, I see. Well, most unfortunate. Yes indeed. To explain, he recently discovered he had relations in New York . . .' Chadwick paused a moment, 'correction, by recently I mean within the last eighteen months. Indeed, we did the research.'

Jim leaned forward. 'The hell's that got to do with me?' he growled.

'Clearly he did not tell you,' Chadwick said. 'He changed his will, Mr Alston. The ranch, the whole kit and caboodle, goes to his wife's relatives, but he did leave you five hundred dollars as recompense for all you meant to him over the years and all you did for him.'

His wife, Sarah, had relations? Jim pondered. She came from back East. Postal wife. Mort married her soon as she got off the coach. Jim sat up straight in his chair, stunned.

'Why, that low-down son of a bitch!' he breathed.

Then suspicion flooded through him and he added, 'I don't believe it. Show me the proof, goddamn you!'

Chadwick bowed his head slightly.

'Of ourse, but first I will ask you to moderate your language.'

'You will hell!' growled Jim. 'Now git to it.'

Chadwick lifted up a briefcase that was placed next to his chair. He opened it and lifted out a sheaf of papers.

'It is all here, Mr Alston,' he said. 'You will see Mr Basset's signature is at the bottom. All legal and above board, I assure you.'

His hands now trembling, Jim read the document. Sure enough, it was like Chadwick said, and Mort's signature was at the bottom. He could not mistake it.

A lump that felt like ice settled in his stomach. After near twenty-five years of close friendship, greater than that between two brothers maybe. Had it all been a callous sham?

Had Mort just used him like some goddamned mule? Worked him near to the bone sometimes, just to build up Slash B and to hell with Jim Alston?

Jim let the news sink in; he found it was the bitterest pill he'd ever had to swallow, but swallow it he did. He was built that way; it was just another knock in a life full of knocks. He would get over it.

'What about my job?' he said, calm now.

'Ah, yes,' said Chadwick. 'I'm afraid my clients want to put their own man in. I'm truly sorry, Mr Alston.'

Jim stared at the man. There did seem to be a smidgen of sincerity about him. 'Yes,' he said. 'Strange as it might seem, I do believe you are.'

He got up to leave but Chadwick raised a hand.

'About the five hundred dollars, Mr Alston; I can get it out of the bank, but you will need to sign.'

Jim stared at him for some seconds, then he said,

'You got worthwhile charities in New York?'

'Of course,' Chadwick replied.

'You choose,' said Jim. 'Give it to them.'

Chadwick looked surprised. He seemed undecided for a moment, but then ducked his head slightly and said,

'As you wish, but you will need to sign papers to that effect.'

'All legal and aboveboard, huh?' Jim said. 'Make them up and I'll sign. Good day to you, sir.'

Chadwick rose from his chair with him and extended his hand.

'I hope this has not been too great a shock,' he said. Jim took his hand and shook it.

'I'll live with it,' he said.

Chadwick nodded, his stare was penetrating.

'Yes, I believe you will,' he said. 'Indeed, I'm sure you will. I can only wish you good fortune, sir.'

Jim let him show him through the now open door. But out on the street he stared at the sky and heaved a huge sigh.

Then he thought: *the hell with it*!

CHAPTER TWENTY-ONE

He rode back to Slash B, picked up his possibles and returned to Broken Mesa. Now he was sitting with Dolly Grover in her pink frilly parlour, drinking good sipping whiskey and with a huge beefsteak and crisp potato fries digesting easily in his belly. He swirled the whiskey in his glass and looked at the love of his life.

'I need a job, beautiful,' he said.

First thing he'd done was to tell her about the will.

Asking for a job now caused her to bark and give him her most severe look.

'You should have listened to me, Jim Alston. I told you to leave that man years ago.

Jim lifted dark brows, nodded. 'Yup, you did say that . . . and often.'

Dolly's wrath left her. She leaned over and clasped his empty hand, hugging it to her warm right cheek.

'Oh, Jim, what an awful thing for that man to do.'

Jim shrugged. 'Deep down, that was Mort, I guess. Just

taken a long time for me to realize it.'

Dolly nestled her head against his chest.

'About that other business you were on, the one con-cerning the Freemans you talked about, your trip to Cheyenne and what you found out there.'

Jim looked into pale amber drink, pursed his lips.

'Sometimes a man has to make his own judgement, Dolly. I've made mine. Case closed.'

'How about Dixon?'

'Got a gut feelin' he looks at it in a similar way. Strange man, Dixon.'

Dolly leaned back, looked deeply into his eyes.

'Not the only strange man hereabouts,' she said, 'but the one I'm talking about I love to bits. And regarding that job you were asking about, I've bought out the Trailman's Rest and I'm lookin' for a fella' to run it. How you fixed?'

Jim stared at her. Dammit if she weren't the most enter-prising woman in all Broken Mesa. What had he been thinking of all these years? He shook his head, leaned for-wards and looked into Dolly's smiling eyes.

'You know, honey bunch, I've got to be the luckiest man in the world,' he said. Then he kissed her, long and hard. When he finally let her go she said,

'Jees, it's late and I'm tired. Carry me to bed will you, Jim, please.' She smiled. 'By the way, I put clean sheets on only this morning you'll be glad to hear.'

Dammit, thought Jim, what could a man do but accede to his one love's wishes. He downed the last of his whiskey, picked Dolly up as though she was a feather and gently carried her upstairs. Inside the bedroom he kicked the door closed. A bright moon shone through the lacy nets that Dolly had at her window.

Not like looking out on the big prairie and pushing beeves, thought Jim, but it would do.

Age was catching him up.